TRAPPED AWAKENING

TRAPPED AWAKENING

RESTLESS DREAMS

B. B. B.

Paperback Edition ISBN: 979-8-9916636-0-1

Published by B.B.B.
bbbwriterbbb@gmail.com

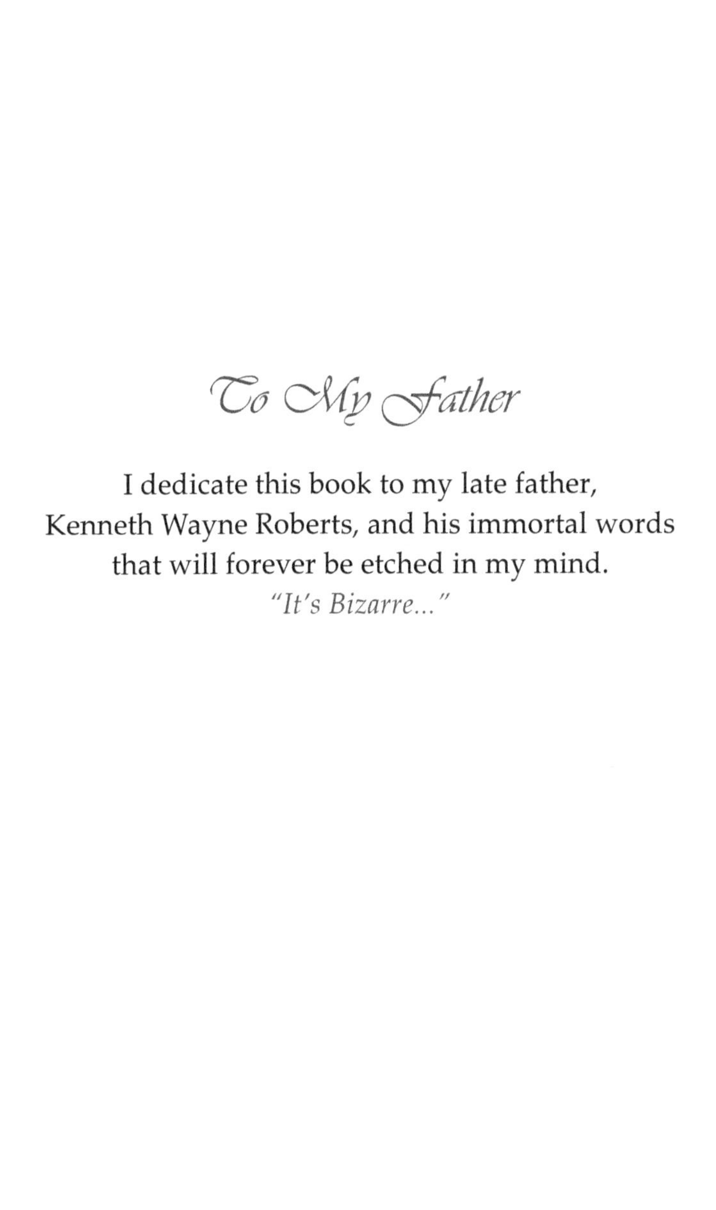

To My Father

I dedicate this book to my late father,
Kenneth Wayne Roberts, and his immortal words
that will forever be etched in my mind.
"It's Bizarre..."

Table of Contents

Introduction

As a lucid dreamer, I learned early on there were locked doors in the human brain that one day modern science will hopefully be able to unlock. I was able to unlock one of these doors with the key of the subconscious. As I slept, I painted my own canvas of reality and wove in what details suited me best. After all, it was my dream and I was in charge, but the more skilled of an oneironaut (someone who travels within dreams) I became, the more my nights were plagued by nightmares and night terrors that would bleed over into my waking world. Until one night I went on a different journey altogether – an out-of-body experience that would change me forever and is one of the main inspirations for this story.

I wrote this book in the most uncertain time of my life. Struggling with depression and newfound sobriety, I couldn't help but dive headfirst into those burning questions we all ask at some point in our limited time we spend on this earth. God, the universe, life, purpose, and understanding were all crammed into the forefront of my mind while I pieced myself back together after a decade of self-abuse. Jobless and unsure of what the future might hold, I began to write. Although I had zero experience in the literary world, Trapped Awakening began to write itself, as if it was supposed to be written.

Journey with me into the mind of an ordinary man who is about to discover life is not what it seems. Reality as he knows it will become unhinged and change forever, and he will soon realize that he is part of something much greater than himself. Desperate for answers, Kevin must stick to the path set beneath his feet if he is to preserve what sanity he has left. With a little help and determination, he will learn just how much the human mind is capable of and how fragile it is…

Chapter 1
Occupational Hazards

Restless dreams, now and then,
Up the ladder and down again.

He looked up and wondered at the beauty of the stars. They twinkled and danced across the sky like fireflies, shining and swaying from one side of the black canvas to the next where the moon rested. His body emanated a radiant aura, casting a purple glow on the cool sands beneath his feet. "What is this place?" he asked aloud. A trickling of water could be heard in the distance, but it was magnified and echoed from far off in the darkness like a leaky faucet at the end of a long hallway. As he examined the stars above, they worked together to form distinct images that he felt a strange connection to like deja vu. A mighty oak, with its sprawling branches and broad trunk, was suspended in the star-lit canvas. *This is beautiful!* he thought as he stared at the mural and pondered its meaning. Before his eyes, the branches of the tree dropped their starry leaves and transformed into a massive set of antlers that crowned the head of a mystic Deer.

Awe-struck and confused by the projections, he continued to gaze at the skyscape, which shifted focus to the moon. The stars swirled and surrounded the glowing orb, creating an upper and lower ridge. The ridges connected and formed the lid and lashes of a giant eye, staring back down at him. Convinced he was in the presence of a higher power, he fell to his knees in bewilderment. The eye slowly closed and then reopened to reveal the moon had turned a red hue. *Oh no…* he thought, as a sense of unease and uncertainty came over him.

A low frequency vibration came from the sands as the grains started to bounce off of one another, building to a steady quake. An unnatural breeze began pushing him into the air, along with the sands around him. His face was frozen in a statue-like look of terror – he couldn't even breathe as he began rising faster through the air. Looking up, the stars glowed brighter and began falling to the earth, zooming past him like glowing golf balls. They crashed into the ground in flashes of blue light, melting patches of the sand into purple glass bowls that now peppered the landscape. Faster and faster he was rocketed into space. The cosmos passed him by as he headed toward the ominous red eye above. It began to close once more, and he closed his.

Kevin inhaled deeply after being jarred awake. "What time is it?" he asked, catching a glimpse of the back light of Katie's phone. She was already awake, but Kevin felt like he could have used another hour or two of rest. He was about to start a new job on what felt like fumes. The fragments of a peculiar dream were still floating around in his head, but the harder he tried to remember, the faster the memory spiraled down the drain of his mind.

"It's three o'eight," she said as Kevin rolled toward her with a disgruntled sigh. Sleeping was beginning to feel more like a chore in the busy lives they had carved out for themselves. Work, eat, bathe, sleep, and repeat turned out to be the magic formula as of late.

"This isn't fair," Kevin moaned. He had to be up at four so he could make it on time for his first day on the job. A dull ache pulsed up his neck and settled at the base of his skull. Nothing new here, a migraine had become a regular part of Kevin's life, rearing its ugly head once every three or four days. Holding good posture and steady ibuprofen use were the only things that kept them at bay, far enough for him to function at least.

Their faithful companion Boone was draped over Kevin's legs, clearly having no problem maintaining his slumber. This pit bull was nothing more than a big baby. All he wanted out of life was their unconditional love and attention, so naturally he hated to watch them leave in the morning. If he had his way, the three of them would never leave the comfort of home, and of course, an increase in table scraps would be in order. "I just had a weird dream, I don't remember much, but it's the first time I've remembered one since I was a kid," Kevin said to Katie, as he propped one arm under his chin.

"Yeah? What happened? Maybe you should write it down like you used to," she replied.

"It's all pretty fuzzy… not enough to put into words. All I remember was standing barefoot on a beach at night, and the stars were beautiful," Kevin answered.

"Hmm… that sounds more romantic than strange; was I there?" she asked.

"No, just me this time," he replied with a grin.

"Bummer! I've been dying to stick my toes in the sand. Why don't you make us some coffee, hun? I'm tired of lying here," she said as she sat upright in the bed and turned the TV on.

"Yes, dear..." Kevin replied, and his seemingly lifeless corpse slithered toward the foot of the bed. The glare on the TV was blinding as his feet finally planted themselves on the knotty pine floor of their bedroom. The news channel didn't waste any time spewing its regular load of half-truths and full-blown lies. "Cartoons make more sense," he said under his breath as he shuffled toward the kitchen. Katie chuckled and yawned with a roar that would rival a lion.

"Hazelnut coffee is running low, babe, and there are a few other things we should grab from the store. Do you want me to swing by after work? Or can you take care of it?" Kevin shouted from the kitchen as the coffee maker finally started to percolate.

"I'll take care of it, hun, I'm off early today," she said.

Kevin's eyes opened wide, and his bottom lip curled in dramatic fashion. "Lucky!" he exclaimed. She had been working a lot of hours at the office and the overtime cap for the week had been met, so Kevin made peace with the fact that she had earned her brief reprieve from the hustle and bustle of their never-ending rat race, although the envy was still written all over his face. When the coffee finished, the smell was breathing life into him once more. He poured two cups and returned to the bedroom, handed his wife her fair share of the bounty, and took a seat at the foot of the bed in front of the TV.

By the grace of God, Katie had changed the channel and Kevin was grateful to see a familiar wascally wabbit creating mischief and mayhem for a bumpkin and his boom-stick. The first sip of joe scalded the tip of his tongue, as it always managed to do, but Kevin was a glutton for punishment, at least that's what his grandmother always used to say. "Do you want to shower first? Or can I?" Katie asked as the mug slowly approached her lips. He didn't bother warning her about the blazing manna that had recently boiled his taste buds, she had common sense and they both knew it. Kevin raised an arm and took a brief and reserved whiff.

"You go ahead, I can make it till this evening," he said as she looked at him with eyes of disdain. She rolled those beautiful eyes he had fallen in love with and headed to the bathroom with her mug still in hand. It was refreshing for him to remember how lucky he was from time to time, because he had been gifted an angel.

After gathering the daily essentials – phone, keys, wallet, etc. – Kevin finished getting dressed and took a squat on their perfectly worn-out couch to put his work boots on. He had high hopes for the new position he would be filling at a young construction company that had recently branched into their area.

It would be a lie to say his nerves weren't dancing like a cat on a hot tin roof, and the caffeine was fuel for the fire. The night before, Kevin made sure the truck was clean and stocked with hardware. He organized the toolboxes to check off the basics needed for any day one blue collar job. Measuring tape, speed square, box cutter, and pencil were all in his tool belt laying in the passenger seat ready to go. Nevertheless, there was still the lingering feeling of forgetfulness buzzing around his head, as always.

Boone came up to him, staring with a look of absolute sorrow. He could tell daddy was about to go back to work after being home for the last few weeks and the extra playtime was at an end. He walked to the back door and turned to Kevin, expecting him to use what he thought was witchcraft to open the portal-gateway that led to the wilderness realm. In the twirling of Kevin's thoughts, he had almost forgotten to let Boone out and feed him. He was a baby, but an eighty pound baby with muscles and claws, and not feeding him usually led to whining and crankiness. The door swung open, and Boone burst forth to relieve himself for the first time since the previous evening.

Kevin stepped out onto the patio to keep an eye on him and take a deep breath of the crisp morning air. The sun was still tucked behind the trees, and finding it meant beginning his day that he had been dreading thus far. In a strange way, the sound of the crickets and the soft breeze sailing by gave him the feeling that everything was going to be okay. Boone scratched at the turf and took off with his victory tradition of a few full speed laps around the yard before returning to gobble his breakfast.

Katie was still in the bathroom getting ready, but she didn't need to leave until six. It was showtime, and the only thing left to do was hit the road. Kevin popped his head in the bathroom for his farewell and good luck kiss for courage. With that, he headed toward the door. "Don't forget your lunch box!" Katie shouted just before he pulled the door closed behind him. To his delight, Kevin hustled back to the kitchen and found it on the counter. Not only had he forgotten to grab his lunchbox, he hadn't even put one together, but in her infinite wisdom, the lady of the castle managed to conjure up a good ole cheese sandwich without him even noticing. Another reason she was his angel.

Kevin gave his thanks and ran out the door. The distinct sound of Boone slamming into the couch to get one last look at him before he rode off into the sunrise reverberated through the wall and echoed down the driveway. Kevin chuckled and waved at him before climbing into the truck. A quick prayer, "Lord, keep your hands on me today," then he turned the key and put it in gear.

The road was damp, and the neighbor's solar lamps shined through a layer of dew resting on their perfectly groomed zoysia lawn, reflecting a dull white glow on the surface. For a brief moment, his brain had been tricked into believing it had snowed in the middle of June. As he pulled away, it reminded him of how envious he was. Cutting the lawn was a therapeutic pastime of his, but Kevin couldn't afford to sow a hybrid super turf and pour thousands of dollars into yearly maintenance, maybe one day. It was four-thirty, and it wasn't going to take much longer to get to the shop, though early was always better in his opinion.

The dull ache in the base of Kevin's skull was slowly transforming into a steady throbbing. Cervicogenic headaches were a common occurrence since he was a kid due to an accidental neck injury roughhousing with the guys, but a few painkillers and a bit of caffeine made short work of them. These bad boys left untreated, however, could bring the strongest of men to their knees in tears. Kevin popped a few pills from a bottle he had stashed in the glovebox for emergencies, and the half gallon of coffee running through his veins was doing a good job of keeping it tolerable. The illuminated street sign reading the words *Hearth and Slab Construction and Design* was approaching on the right.

It was a thrilling "too good to be true"

concept for a company specializing in rustic design to just appear seemingly out of thin air. It was right up his alley, and the enjoyment of working with rough cut lumber had been sorely missed for the past few years. Everything up to this point had been repetitive paint tones, cheap flooring, and generic trim styles. Kevin pulled down the short gravel road that led to an open parking area filled with heavy equipment and vehicles that seemed to be clean and well maintained, which was a refreshing change of pace. A few guys were already loading their tools into a massive tank of a work van.

He parked and grabbed his tools, hopped out, and headed over to introduce himself. "Hey, fellas, I'm Kevin – the new guy," he said hastily.

"James; nice to meet you," one of them said.

"Bobby," another greeted with a handshake.

"You're not going to need that shit today," the third said with the undeniable odor of breakfast beer and cigarettes on his breath.

Great, Kevin thought to himself, *there's always that guy*. "What do you mean?" Kevin asked as they continued to load more of the tools he assumed they would need for the day.

"We're going to a big remodel today, and you're the new guy, which means you get to pull cedar siding all day."

"Damn," Kevin muffled under his breath;

this was not what he had in mind for day one. Kevin didn't care to get Sir Smokes-a-lot's real name at this point, and he clearly didn't care to give it. Demo was usually straight-forward, brainless work, but ripping down cedar siding was always a miserable process. Using a crow's foot to pry at half-brittle, half-rotten cedar boards that split apart, dropping cranky carpenter bees rudely awakened from their nap and dust that would choke a jet engine, only to discover thousands of nails remaining in the plywood that still need to be pulled by hand. The thoughts cluttered Kevin's mind; nevertheless, he threw his tool belt into the back of the van and took a seat in the rear row. Another guy walked out of the office and jumped in the passenger seat, which prompted the rest of the employees to saddle up and off they went.

"Hey, Bobby, where we gettin' beers tonight? Rick's? Or just swinging by the gas station again?" asked James.

"Probably Rick's, if the new guy does well enough. What do you say, Kevin? Want to grab a drink with us after work?" Bobby replied.

"I don't drink anymore, thanks for the offer though." Kevin responded.

He could tell from the small talk and typical before-work gab in the van that there was truly only one jerk here, and his name was Sir Smokes-a-lot.

Knighted by Jack Daniels himself, he questioned the religious beliefs of the one Hispanic member of the crew, called the guy in front of Kevin an idiot for rooting for the wrong football team, and interrupted every other sensible conversation attempted in the van, complete with racist undertones. It had been ten minutes, and it wasn't even five in the morning yet. Kevin cringed every time the ogre opened his gingivitis-ridden mouth, but it was day one, and calling this guy out on his abhorrent behavior would ultimately lead to trading blows, and it wasn't worth losing this golden opportunity.

The van came to a stop in the cul-de-sac of an older subdivision that had three houses on it. It didn't take long to figure out the house on Haunted Hill was the obvious objective for the day. The other two recently received facelifts and would look picture perfect if it wasn't for the rundown, ramshackle souring the frame. Kevin didn't waste any time jumping out of the van, and James was already pulling an extension ladder from atop the van for him to use. Kevin grabbed a pry bar and headed over to the wall where James leaned the ladder. "Thanks, dude, this is going to suck," Kevin said.

James laughed, "I know, I figured you're going to be up there all day so the least I can do is move the ladder for you." James had just earned the title of favorite coworker in Kevin's book, and rightly so. With a slow, deep breath of tolerance, he put on his gloves and started the climb.

Board by board, nail by nail, he toiled away at the daunting task at hand. Hours had passed and only a few square feet of siding remained on the south-east side of the house. It reminded Kevin of a time he worked with his father on an old camper when he was just seven years old. For a moment, he reminisced on the memory. His father handed him a screw gun and taught him how to use it safely, then handed him a box of galvanized hex-head screws. The camper was trimmed with chrome strips that were held on by rusty self-tappers. His mission was to replace the old rusty hardware with the new screws, but as a kid, Kevin didn't see it as such a daunting task, even though there were close to a thousand screws holding it together. It didn't feel like work; he was just having fun with dad.

The heat of the June sun snapped him back to reality. Now only about nine, it was starting to get unreasonably hot. Sweat was falling like rain, and before long he was soaked. As soon as a fresh bottle of water had been consumed, an equal volume of liquid was expelled through his pores. Working by himself on one task at a time was actually the way he preferred to labor, so there was no room for complaint. Heavy breathing and aching muscles were welcome signs that it was time for a quick break, so Kevin hung his crow bar on a rung of the ladder and proceeded to descend his post.

Sweating profusely had not only soaked him but the rungs of his ladder as well, and a shallow step with just the toe of his boot caused such a slip that reaffirming a grip on the rungs was impossible. Kevin was going down and going down fast. When you stay twenty-five feet high for that long, you tend to forget just how high twenty-five feet really is. His chin took a blow from the next step down that felt like a knockout uppercut from Iron Mike Tyson and sent him hurtling backwards toward the earth like a meteor. It was as if Kevin had all the time in the world to examine every mistake he had ever made up to this point in close detail. Not being a better husband, failing to call his grandmother on a more regular basis, and even neglecting to throw a tennis ball for Boone everyday crossed his mind. Kevin's body plummeted to the ground in two seconds and **BAM!** Like a limp ragdoll, his seemingly lifeless corpse collided with the soil, echoing a thud that could be heard from inside the house.

All at once, the ground tore away at itself from underneath Kevin, and he continued to fall. The sod and sediment of the earth had opened up a swallowing abyss that he feared would surely become his grave, but he felt no pain and fell farther. The screams couldn't escape his lips as sheer terror kept his lungs empty and his blood ran cold with fear. A violent tug at his ankle cracked every vertebra in his spine and slammed him into the wall of the bottomless cavern. By the grace of God, he had become tangled in a large root system that gave way when the massive chasm unlatched. Helpless, Kevin dangled with no attempt at movement. There was still no pain, even though his mouth was filling with blood; his tongue was partially severed and he knew that he should be in anguish. Tears began to fill Kevin's eyes – although he was still alive, the possibility of paralysis was the only thought left in his mind.

Slowly swinging from left to right and spinning ever so slightly, the dust and debris settled around him and his sight returned. The light shining down from the sky into the opening of the cave could be seen in patches past the roots and rubble. A faint voice rang out, "Kevin?! KEVIN?! Are you okay?" It was James. Though he couldn't respond, Kevin could see James' shadow peering over the edge, and he barely made out, "Help is coming, buddy! Hold on!" This glimmer of hope allowed him to gather his thoughts and take stock of the situation.

He could blink but could barely breathe. *Maybe a collapsed lung?* he thought, but blood was rushing to Kevin's head faster than he could think.

His clothes, arms, and neck were caked in a layer of dust clinging to the sweat he was still soaked with. *What the hell just happened? Is this a sinkhole?* Kevin asked himself. The welcome feeling of his fingertips bending back and forth granted some relief because at least that meant he wasn't completely paralyzed. The absence of pain was still worrisome, he was trapped deep in the earth, and passing out was a likely possibility from hanging upside down for too long.

Like a mangled marionette with no master, gravity spun Kevin around to reveal something he hadn't noticed yet. The extension ladder had fallen as well and wedged itself diagonally in the crevice underneath. *Oh good, it followed me,* Kevin thought to himself as a humorous grunt left his throat and gave way to a stream of blood trickling toward his forehead. He looked up one more time and noticed another silhouette looking down at him, but this one was silent, motionless, and much, much darker. Kevin's heartbeat slowed. There was absolute silence above and below, and the air was surprisingly cool and fresh. Stillness and calm overtook him as his eyes closed.

Chapter 2
Dazed and Confused

The mind splits, one becomes two,
Reality in question, now who is who?

"Kevin, wake up… Kevin, d'ya hear that?" the man said as Kevin opened his eyes. Groggy and disheveled, he looked around and noticed a strange, ragged man on the other side of a smoldering campfire that gave off just enough light to illuminate his presence. Tightly gripping a bolt-action hunting rifle, he was clearly unnerved by something. They were alone in the middle of a swampy jungle path, surrounded by tropical brush on either side. "Listen!" the man whispered, as he stared farther down the dismal path.

"I don't hear any… wait," the words barely

made it out of Kevin's mouth before the eerie sound of movement came from somewhere off the path. The hairs stood up on the back of their necks, as the skulking of something large got closer and closer.

"What do we do... It's right on top of us!" the man stuttered over his words as he raised the barrel of his weapon and pointed it at where he thought the sounds were coming from.

Kevin responded, "Stay quiet... stay still." The two of them sat petrified in silence as the unknown lurked merely feet away. It was coming from the scruffy man's side of the path. Twigs snapped and branches of tropical leaves broke as something big inched its way toward them. Loud and aggressive snorts of exhale could be heard just on the other side of the jungle brush.

"Shit!!!" the man shrieked in terror and took off running into the darkness, leaving his rifle in the mud.

"WAIT! STOP!" Kevin shouted, but the man was already long gone, and the beast was upon him. Frozen in time, he watched in horror as the glowing embers illuminated the tips of pointed bones slowly protruding from the vegetation. It reached for him across the path, like a giant skeletal hand, as the sound of snorting continued. His heartbeat and breath were on pause as the finger-like bones slowly tilted upward, revealing the face of a massive Deer.

Its mouth opened, and shouted with a thunderous echo, *WAKE UP!*

"Honey, get up, you're going to be late!" The words jolted Kevin into an upright position. He was soaked in a cold sweat with yet another throbbing headache to start his day.

"What a dream," he whispered as Katie made her way through the room already dressed, which meant he was way behind.

"You must not have set your alarm," she said.

"There I go, failing to complete crucial daily life tasks again," he responded. In a whirlwind, Kevin got dressed, grabbed his lunchbox – which Katie remembered to pack for him yet again – took a quick chug from the milk carton and scarfed a muffin. To his dismay, as he chewed, he noticed a sore spot on the side of his tongue, but it wasn't uncommon for him to get a canker sore or eat too fast, resulting in an uncomfortable next few days. "Almost late on day two wouldn't look great," he whimpered to Katie. She gave him a furrowed brow look as he leaned in for his ritual good luck kiss.

"You're not late yet, just don't stop for donuts," she laughed as he hurried out the door.

Kevin took two steps and froze. The blood in his veins ran cold and the hairs on his arms shot up.

A wave of confusion came over him because it just occurred to him that he had no recollection of the previous evening. This was seriously concerning – he was used to forgetting what was for dinner the night before, but he had never lost an entire block of time. Could the dream of falling off the ladder be real? Convincing himself there was a logical explanation, he knew there wasn't any time to dwell on it, so he got in his truck and headed for the shop. As he rumbled down the highway a tad faster than usual, Kevin thought of the dream he had and the fact that it was the only reference to any memory of the day before, but it was still just a dream.

Something must have happened that caused him to forget, like heat exhaustion or a concussion. "That's it!" he shouted out loud. He must have actually fallen off that ladder and hit his head, which would explain the headache, but Kevin ran his fingers through his hair and couldn't locate a bump. His mind was relatively set at ease as he pulled into the gravel parking lot. All the familiar faces were jumping into the van and he had made it on time, which was a big relief.

"Look who showed up," barked the curmudgeon as Kevin approached the van. He walked past and didn't say a word, he wasn't worth Kevin's breath or time. A sly grin appeared on his scruffy, sunbaked face as if he had some demented sense of success at crawling under his skin.

James was already seated in the middle row, and he was the only guy pleasant enough to converse with, so Kevin sat next to him. Knowing very well that eventually he was going to have to ask someone about the gaps in his memory, James seemed to be the best candidate. Now to orchestrate the question in a way that didn't point straight to lunacy. "Hey James, I need some advice. Do you think I did enough yesterday? I feel like I didn't pull my weight," Kevin asked in order to fish for more information. James' answer brought an all too familiar chill to his blood.

"First of all, Thomas, my name is Eric, and second, I think you did better than the new guy at the very least. He didn't make it three hours before falling off that ladder, remember?"

Kevin's eyes widened before turning to the front of the van. Now there was a whole swath of questions, begging to be asked. He would have sworn on his father's grave that the man he was speaking to told him his name was James. Not to mention, his name was Kevin and wasn't he the new guy that fell off the ladder? "Is he okay?" he asked in a sunken tone.

The man replied, "He got up pretty quick and walked away from it, so I'm assuming he's fine. I think his wife came to pick him up."

What the hell is going on? he thought. *Could*

this be some elaborate prank planned on the spot because I hit my head? If so, they had him hook, line and sinker, because an explanation simply couldn't be put into words. He prayed to God that it was a joke; if it wasn't, then that meant he was in serious need of some form of medical treatment.

Kevin could see them playing off a legitimate case of amnesia. He looked around the van for the man who called himself Bobby the day before, but he was nowhere in sight. He could have called out of work, and all that was left was for James to claim a different name and convince Kevin his name wasn't Kevin. He might've been onto something if it wasn't for the sinkhole, and surely Katie wouldn't let him leave the house after sustaining a memory altering head trauma. There was no clear choice but to stay quiet and play along. For all he knew, this was still day two and causing a scene by calling them out on their shenanigans probably wouldn't go well for anyone, especially if it wasn't a prank. He'd be thrown in the looney bin for sure.

The van came to an abrupt halt in the same cul-de-sac as before, but all Kevin wanted to do was go home, curl up into a ball and contemplate his own existence. There was a job to do before he could. "Just get through this," he said under his breath while the crew began reporting to their assigned tasks. The pry bar was staring him down from the back of the van,

and all he needed to do was continue the exterior demo. This kind of work could flip the autopilot switch, making it easier to toil the day away and get home. Kevin went to work, still pondering the possibility that he could be finally losing my mind.

No more than forty-five minutes later, the racist ogre approached from around the corner of the house. "What are you doing?" he asked with a genuinely confused sway in his voice. Kevin's patience was running thin, and the stress of a serious psychological condition was taking its toll on his mood and emotions.

"What does it look like I'm doing?" he snapped without even looking in his direction.

"Woah! Somebody's cranky today! You're supposed to be finishing the oak beams. They've got to be hung by Friday." His tone wasn't nearly as sarcastic as the day before. Kevin couldn't take any more surprises, but he had to admit he was curious about the beams he was talking about. He turned and lumbered back the way he came so Kevin followed. If he had to switch gears for the day, at least he was familiar with rustic beams, faux or authentic. It was the work he loved.

Walking across the dilapidated front porch was a feat in itself. Plywood had been laid over an opening in the rotten boards that had collapsed. The front door had been taken off the hinges to make more room for hauling tools and the compressor into the house. This building was old, like colonial old, and unreasonably out of place. Passing through the doorway revealed a saloon style open concept with a ceiling that felt thirty feet high. Balconied walkways wrapped three of the walls not including the front of the house and two narrow ornate stairways hugged the walls on either side of the front door. He could see multiple doors on the second floor he assumed were bedrooms. There in front of him rested one massive faux oak beam on a set of sawhorses accompanied by four smaller beams and a stack of one-by-eight oak border boards, mostly stained in a beautiful custom walnut and mahogany mix.

The place had charm, that much was certain. Through the peeling wallpaper and bowing floorboards, a blank canvas could be seen, and Kevin had the ability to paint that canvas in his mind the way he saw fit. The finished product would be a masterpiece. He passed the palms of his callused hands over the coarse surface of the sawmill style beams. *Did I really make these?* He couldn't believe the words crossing his mind, but a part of him wanted to believe it because they were perfect. Kevin felt proud of something he probably had nothing to do with, but for a split second, it was a welcome distraction from the rest of what was cluttering his memory cache. He took a breath of musty air and grabbed a rag along with the jar of stain mix, and autopilot engaged.

Hours later, they were headed back to the shop, and Kevin couldn't have been more relieved. Mentally, emotionally, and physically exhausted, his mood boosted at the sight of his pickup as they rolled into the gravel lot.

Before he could make a clean getaway, "Eric," or whatever that guy's name was, grabbed a hold of his truck door and asked if he was okay. "Hey, Thomas, are you feeling alright? You've looked like you've seen a ghost all day. You're pale as ale," he questioned Kevin mid-climb into the driver seat.

Half of Kevin wanted to flip "Eric" the bird and slam his fingers in the door. He made direct eye contact with him and said, "I definitely feel like one." The answer couldn't have been more accurate, but something about him just walking away pushed Kevin over the edge. He couldn't keep it to himself any longer. "Hey, come back for just a second. I've got a question," he said. The man returned to the side of his truck as he continued. "You guys are screwing with me, right? I mean I get it, new guy at work, first day and all. You gotta mess with him. I fell off that ladder, and I must have hit my head hard because I can't remember anything afterwards. You guys really had me going, I've got to admit, but it's seriously starting to stress me out so please come clean with me."

Eric just stared with serious concern in his eyes and said, "I think you should go home and get some rest, Thomas. A belly full of food and a good night's rest would do you a world of good." He just walked away without a second thought, seemingly unaware that Kevin's perspective on reality was crumbling around him.

"My name is not Thomas…" Kevin whispered to himself. He was alone, or at least that was how he had felt all day. The only solace he expected to find was in the arms of his loving wife. Surely she would be able to help in some way.

During his silent drive home, he battled with how to break the news to Katie about what had been happening to him. *How can I even begin to explain this to her? What if she thinks I'm just faking to get out of work? Will she still love me if I lose my mind?* He tried to anticipate the possible reactions before pulling in the driveway. He knew he needed help, but he had no idea how to ask for it. Kevin clung to the hope that this was all some sort of well thought out buffoonery, but unlikely. His heavy work boots trudged through the front door with a new weight to them that Katie picked up on right away. She was lying on the couch with the fur baby when a look of concern filled her eyes.

"You look like you've had a terrible day,

honey," is all she had time to say before a solitary tear started rolling down Kevin's left cheek, and it took a few minutes before he could even speak without choking on the words. Part of him was still clinging to a splinter of hope that she would spill the beans about his co-workers prank and that she was in on it the whole time. Kevin simply knew better.

"I need to go to the doctor," left his lips in a quiet tone. The concern deepened in her eyes as he continued. "I've lost a large chunk of memory. I remember falling off a ladder yesterday, and my coworkers have been messing with my mind, or at least I hope they were. I need you to tell me anything you know about yesterday." Confusion had fully replaced concern at this point.

"It was a fairly normal day from what I can remember, although you did seem a bit more distant than usual. Tell me what's going on."

"Distant? What exactly does that mean?" Kevin inquired.

She responded, "Well, for a first day of work at a new job, you didn't mention much about it. I normally get my ear talked off regardless if it turned out good or bad and you had this zoned out look on your face. I assumed you were just really tired." A sigh of relief bellowed from his lungs. Kevin was back to being the new guy and that was almost all he needed to hear to reaffirm that those jerks had played him for a fool.

"Okay, that makes more sense. I didn't mean to worry you, my love. I'm convinced this has all been a practical joke. I'm going to let the dog out and grab a quick shower, and I'll tell you more before bed," he said.

Boone must have heard what he said, he was already reporting for duty at the back door. The air outside had cooled, and for the last couple of weeks, the dark hours of the day had been surprisingly comfortable, given what time of year it was. Boone trotted around, sniffing at his favorite spots, while Kevin took a seat in one of the patio chairs. It was nice to finally catch a breather and unwind after such a horrible day. A deep breath helped calm the nerves. He closed his eyes and focused on his breathing to disband the clutter in his head. The fragments of the dream Kevin had the night before made him wonder if his memory issue could be related to the strange dreams he used to have when he was younger. The sky was clear, and the moonlight beamed down and lit up the area where Boone was finishing his business.

The dirty clothes started hitting the floor in the hallway, piece by piece. He almost stepped into the shower with his socks still on and without giving ample time to let the water warm up. Kevin's body was locked in place, with head hung low, allowing the cleansing stream to rinse the stress of the day away. He was home, in his safe haven, and a part of him knew everything was going to be okay. There was still no explanation for the lack of head injury however, and what was the sinkhole all about? A few suds and the stroke of a toothbrush later, he walked through the bedroom doorway to find his wife and spoiled-rotten canine already under the covers.

The bedside lamplight revealed she was reading a new novel. *SHERLOCK HOLMES* – he could barely make out the name on the hardback spine while crawling into his side of the bed. Kevin told her about the dream of falling from a ladder into a bottomless pit and his theory on the shenanigans his coworkers had been pulling, including all the name confusion. He finished with, "The weirdest part is that I can't remember the second half of yesterday at all."

She didn't even look up from her book, as if unfazed by all the strange happenings of his day. Her reply, for a third and final time for the day, iced his blood in a way that would make a dead man shiver. "I'll schedule you an appointment with a specialist in the morning, I'm getting worried, Thomas."

Kevin's heart sank into his stomach and there it would lay for the rest of the night. He was Thomas again according to Katie. He was losing his mind, but the saddest part of it all was his wife didn't even

seem to care. His worst fears were coming true. As
he rolled over to conceal the silent weeping, the only
words he could come up with were, "Me, too."

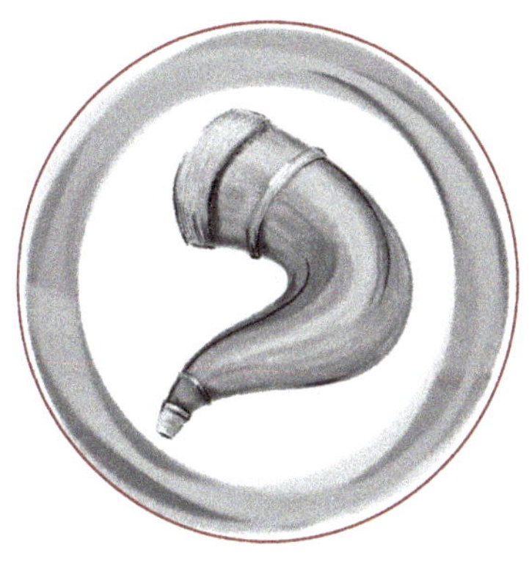

Chapter 3
A Whole New World

A beautiful dream, magnificent sights,
Spectacular scene with sun shining bright.

Agentle wind brushed his cheek. The soothing sound of tall grass swaying in the breeze followed, and the fragrance of wild lavender teased the nostrils. A distant chirp of a seagull above reeled in consciousness. and once again, Kevin was awakened with such force that would have cracked his skull if he were sleeping in a bunk bed. It was as if his soul was reattaching to his body, and his lungs drew in enough air to fill a car tire. Incoherent and coming out of what felt like a drug induced stupor, Kevin's vision slowly revealed a startling scene. Once he was firing on all cylinders, he realized that he was no longer in the comfort of his own bed but somewhere else entirely.

Heart racing and still catching his breath, Kevin's head swiveled from left to right, displaying a gorgeous landscape filled with intricately placed flora and bursting with the color of flowering dogwoods. The sound of waves crashing on a beach could be heard from behind, but directly in front of him in this field of mystery was a solitary Deer. Majestic and triumphant with head held high, he stared at him with a look of intrigue, and Kevin at him, for what felt like an hour. He curled forward to achieve an all-fours position. He was weak, starving, and thirsting to death. His entire body was sore, and it felt like he had hiked twenty miles to get to where he was, but Kevin managed to raise himself to a standing position. The Deer had vanished, but the intrigue remained.

Something is definitely still wrong, he thought as he gazed in awe at this Eden-like painting of a countryside. This time Kevin didn't feel panic or loss of control, those emotions were replaced with a strange sense of contentment and inner peace. It was just natural to feel like everything was going to be okay, and that he was here for a reason, but why? And how? It didn't matter because of the calm that had overtaken him. The sunrays not only warmed his skin but wrapped around him like a blanket and passed through Kevin in a way that felt energizing.

He turned around and focused his attention on the ocean horizon just past the edge of a cliff. A few steps forward and he was looking down at white sands encompassed in coconut trees and golden rays of light shimmering off the wavy surface of an endless sea. The sands seemed to spread and widen to the left of this massive body of water for thousands of miles. It was a barren desert, besides a single cluster of palms off in the distance. A mirage of liquid color spread the blues and greens of the ocean across the sky, like a runny watercolor painting. Although the sun was radiating a comfortable temperature where he was, Kevin could tell it was hotter than blue blazes in that direction.

Amid his exploration, Kevin couldn't help but think of home, and what was happening to him. Only this time he was content with whichever outcome his mind had in store for him next. Then an overwhelming, but necessary contemplation dominated the next few minutes, which might as well have been hours. *Am I dead? Is this the afterlife?* he thought to himself as a new cognizance put his mind at ease. Not only would that theory put an end to his suffering but if this truly was what the other side looked like, then it wasn't half bad and he could get used to it. As Kevin soaked in the beauty of this place, he thought of his wife and one true love being alone. It didn't even muster up the bellowing sadness that could naturally be expected, like that of an individual lying in their deathbed worrying about the well-being of loved ones they are inevitably going to leave behind. It was like he was incapable of negative thoughts or emotions, and this magical realm was healing parts of himself that even he didn't know were wounded.

Kevin was standing on what could easily be the most attractive plateau on earth, which was usually just flatlands and lacking in notable features, according to what he could remember from geography class. Maybe a boulder or two with a few wildflowers to brighten things up, but this one had everything. He took a step back and turned to face the forest across from the grassy meadow he had awakened in. To his left was a hillside that steadily inclined, with a beaten path that zig-zagged upwards. Off in the distance, a horned ram was meandering down the trail toward him at a leisurely pace, with what appeared to be some sort of cargo like saddle bags. The higher he looked, the higher the path led, ultimately ending at the peak of a mountain. The beginnings of snowcaps lay just under a cloud line that surrounded the highest point, undoubtedly frigid, and it was light-years away.

To his right was a hillside with a gentle slope, and its worn path led below through rolling terrain.

It spiraled downwards into a small marshy clearing filled with cattails and lily pads at the bottom and disappeared behind the menacing opening of a mangrove swamp. The overgrown branches hung down over the trail like fangs in the mouth of a rotten beast. It might have been a trick of the brain, but a familiar silent and still silhouette lingered in its opening. *What is that?* Kevin thought to himself as he squinted his eyes, but the longer he stared, the more he wanted to look away. Kevin had definitely seen it before, but where? The figure eventually dissipated, and from that distance, could have easily just been an animal of some sort. Almost every biome on earth had a home here but convincing him that he was still on planet earth would have been a daunting task for any psychiatrist.

The Deer that disappeared when Kevin had risen to his feet left a parting in the tall grass. It was pointed directly at the forest in front of him, so he decided to follow in its footsteps. Among the many plants and flowers, a few shrubs lay on either side of the parted grass. To his delight, the shrubbery ended up being blueberry bushes, and they couldn't have appeared at a more perfect time to satisfy his thirst and hunger. "Oh YES!" he shouted and hurried over to gobble down as many as he could pick. His face-cramming slowed when the sound of a small cowbell approached from the left.

Kevin peered around the bushes with a mouth full of the delicious berries and saw the same ram trotting toward him, only twenty to thirty yards away. The only part he could see above the tall grass was the curly, slate-colored horns adorning his head. When the ram got within a few feet of the bushes, he came to an abrupt stop and gave Kevin the same stare of intrigue the Deer had given. The ram had a series of leather pouches draped over his back that were tied closed with drawstrings. After a few moments of awkwardly staring back at this creature of the mountain, the ram broke eye contact, lowered his head and shoulders, and took a few steps backward. Kevin took a defensive stance thinking, *This guy is about to clobber me!*

Thankfully, his wooly friend was simply repositioning to allow his cargo to gently slide off onto the ground before making his journey all the way back up the mountain path. Kevin took a knee in front of the gift that was given to discover one of the leather sacks was covered in condensation and filled to the brim with ice cold spring water. Emotions of thankfulness and unworthiness passed as he chugged as much as his belly could hold. The weakness, hunger, and thirst he had arrived with were fading fast, and within a few minutes, Kevin's strength had returned. The water bladder in his hand stayed the same weight and seemed to refill

itself after every swig.

The second pouch was much larger, with inner pockets and two straps that could be tied together and worn as a backpack. The third pouch had been buried underneath the second and upon uncovering it, there were two strange shapes sticking out and looked more like a holster. This one had straps as well, and the first item it stowed was the hollowed-out horn of a bison with a brass mouthpiece. Kevin could tell right away what it was because his grandfather had one exactly like it. The same shape, color, and size, all the way down to the chip at the end and scuff in the brass. *Huh?* he thought, *How did this even get here?*

The last time Kevin remembered seeing it, he was nine years old, playing with it in the small barn used for storage and pretending to be a Viking. He had been told time and time again that this horn wasn't a toy and it needed to be treated with respect. Well, needless to say he broke it. Kevin tripped on a shoelace and stumbled right on top of it, cracking it in half. He knew that his grandfather and father would tan his hide for days if they found out, so he had no choice but to bury the evidence in the back underneath the chicken coop. Even being so young, the guilt followed him into adulthood, especially after they both passed away. It was a cherished family heirloom – one Kevin would never inherit.

But here it was, and he was determined to treat it with respect this time.

The second item had a smooth bone handle with a brass pommel on the end. Slowly, his palm wrapped around the ornate grip and pulled it from its sheath. Both hands cradled what was one hell of a knife. Its blade had a groove running from hilt to tip, with a cutaway at the end like a Bowie, and its edge had been sharpened a thousand times the old-fashioned way with a whetstone. Taking stock of everything, it was becoming more and more clear that Kevin was sent to that place for a reason, and that reason was going to involve quite the adventure.

"Well, I'm guessing this stuff is going to come in handy," he said aloud, strapping the water bladder to his left hip and the knife and horn holster to his right. Luckily, Kevin hadn't woken up in his boxer-briefs like he fell asleep in but in his work clothes of cargo pants, t-shirt, and trusty dusty boots. If there be a long road ahead, he was prepared. There were still hundreds of berries to harvest so he picked a bunch and filled one of the inner pockets of his new backpack for later and tied the shoulder straps across his chest. Curious as ever, Kevin's feet were moving faster and faster through the parted grass. *Now where has that Deer run off to?* his heart said to his brain.

Keeping a brisk pace, Kevin hiked to the very edge of that forest and paused. Up to this point, he hadn't considered the possible dangers of what lay ahead. The euphoric effects of the plateau were wearing off and reality (or at least his original perspective of reality) was setting in. *What am I doing? I'm going to get myself killed if I go in there. I've seen this movie before.* His conscience was speaking to him, but Kevin's gut was telling him to keep moving. The sunlight had diminished under the canopy of hundreds of massive oaks and maples, but the path was still illuminated, thanks to a few scrawny branches giving way to a few intermittent beams of light every ten to fifteen feet. A few steps forward and the forest began to breathe around him. A breeze blew past Kevin and halted, only to return further down the path. Something strange lay at the center of this forest. He couldn't put his finger on it, but it was as if a part of himself was already there. Somehow, Kevin knew if he kept walking, he was going to find himself. Over and over the breeze kept a steady cadence with his feet, and a low hum paired with each exhale. Patches of grass were swaying back and forth on either side of the path with the breeze. Kevin's nerves started getting the better of him because this forest felt alive, and he couldn't help but feel like he was marching right into its belly.

After a few hundred feet inwards, he came upon a felled tree lying across the path covered in moss. The vegetation was beginning to encroach from either side and tighten the walkway, and the air was getting thicker. Kevin always loved nature growing up, but humidity was one of those natural phenomena he'd rather do without for the rest of his life. With uncomfortably sticky skin and labored breathing, he decided to rest on the log before moving on. The moss was soft, and the log was wide enough to stretch out on and relax, so Kevin laid the backpack on the ground and removed the gear he had recently acquired. A few moments of effort later he climbed up, laid down, crossed his ankles, and placed his hands behind his head. Although the air was dense, the breathing of the forest cooled his skin and the sound of crickets was making him drowsy. Kevin's eyes watered for a moment; he missed home and the normalcy of his life a few days prior. He missed his wife. He missed his dog.

Kevin's thoughts began to fade as his sight narrowed, when a swift movement caught the corner of his eye. The fattest, meanest looking spider he had ever seen, the size of his palm, decided to make a pitstop on Kevin's belly while crossing the log. He had gray and black fur all over with red stripes on all eight legs, which had more muscle on them than he did. Kevin kept himself frozen except for one hand that slowly lowered from behind his head. With one fell swoop, a mighty swat fell from the heavens and smote his ruin onto Kevin's work shirt.

His skin crawled as oozing innards and twitching legs dripped from his fingers, and it felt like he had broken his own rib with the blow, but the invader had been vanquished.

The calm breathing of the forest immediately converted to a wailing moan from deep within the woods. The leaves twirled and the branches and trunks around him swayed violently from side to side as if a hurricane was approaching. The commotion made Kevin sit up in terror when an unknown force hurled him through the air and dashed his body across a mighty oak. Kevin's broken corpse fell to the earth. Darkness pulled a curtain over his eyes, but not before he witnessed a slender branch reaching down from the canopy with a skeletal hand of twigs and vines.

Kevin's eyes opened. A bright light kept his vision foggy, and the muffled sound of a conversation could be heard, as if underwater. His movements were slow and delayed due to the stupor he found himself in. Sluggishly, the fog began to lift, and he could make out two alien-like beings in front of him trying to get his attention. "Kevin? Can you hear me?" a distant voice rang out. One of the figures got very close and another blinding light flashed across one eye to the next. Kevin was in a medical office and the two beings were a doctor and his wife. As full consciousness returned, a tornado of confusion and distress forced him to panic.

"Don't touch me!" he yelled as he swatted in the doctor's direction. His balance was way off, and it threw him onto the floor with a thud.

Katie rushed to his side and said, "Lie still! It's okay, he's trying to help." Her voice was what calmed him, not the words she spoke.

"I'm calling in an emergency CT," the doctor said as he left the room.

"Where are we, hun?" Kevin whispered in shock.

With a brief pause before her answer, "The hospital, sweety, you've been very sick." He could feel the distress in her voice. A marriage of relief and sadness caused him to weep uncontrollably, although he was home and back to reality, it confirmed his worst fears. It was official. Kevin had fallen off the deep end and didn't even know how to doggie paddle.

"What… what day is it?" he asked in a timid voice, and being the hardest question to ask, he didn't want to hear the answer.

"It's Sunday. You collapsed Wednesday morning and haven't been to work since. You've been mumbling, not making a lot of sense, and going in and out. Can you remember anything at all?" Kevin shook his head and wiped the tears from his face. A week ago, he had lost an afternoon, now four whole days were missing from his memory.

"Am I finally losing it?" he asked.

"I don't think so babe, you're just sick and we are going to get you better, okay?" she replied.

They sat in silence for the next twenty minutes before a nurse knocked on the door and entered with a clipboard in her hand. Her voice was soothing with her introduction, "Hello Mr. and Mrs. Garner, I'm nurse Johanna. Dr. Seigr has called in a few tests to rule out some of the main concerns he has. We've got you scheduled for a CT scan and an MRI to check for any abnormalities, like cancer or signs of a stroke or seizures. Also, unfortunately, we need to perform a spinal tap to make sure meningitis isn't the cause of your episodes." The news wasn't good, but Kevin felt it wasn't bad either, but a "spinal tap" didn't sound like a great deal of fun to him. She continued, "If you're ready, we can take you down to get the CT out of the way." He looked at his wife and she looked back with, *You got this*, in her eyes. He nodded to nurse Johanna and away they went. She insisted Kevin use a wheelchair – he assumed to avoid any possible blackouts. He didn't scoff, but despite the potentially grim circumstances, Kevin couldn't help making a bit of fun.

"I'm only losing my mind, I can still walk,"

he said. The ladies chuckled, but nurse Johanna was not giving in, so he took his seat and they headed toward the elevator. Passing by other hospital rooms, some open doorways were emitting beeping and buzzing noises from the medical devices in use. One had members of a family laughing with the patient about some funny story. Most of the doors were shut, but the last room before the elevator was dark and the only sound coming from it was the depressing groans of someone in serious pain.

They stopped at the end of the hall, and Katie pressed the down button for the elevator. It could be heard approaching from five or six floors away, as the nurse spoke up to break the silence, "You really don't have anything to worry about, you're in good hands with Dr. Seigr. He's truly one of the best." Something about the way she said it made his nerves quiver just a little bit more. A few seconds later, the elevator doors slid open and the three of them boarded. Before they reached their floor, a jolt of searing pain split Kevin's head wide open, and he was blinded by an unnerving vision. It was like a dream. He was driving late at night and could hear the rattling of empty beer cans rolling around on the passenger floorboard. His heart raced as the headlights swayed from left to right across the road and the engine roared louder. Mailboxes and streetlights on either side of the residential road melted into blurred streams of light as he gave it more and more gas. Within seconds, the headlights shined on an object in the middle of the roadway and his truck smashed into it full speed, spraying his face with glass and blood before a loud **BING** snapped him out of it and the elevator doors opened.

"Babe, are you okay?" Katie asked as they rolled out of the elevator.

Kevin rubbed his forehead as the nurse asked, "Are you getting another headache?"

He didn't want to alarm Katie of his vision, or any medical professional for that matter. "Yeah, just another headache... but it's not taking hold. I should be fine," he answered. A few hallways later, they arrived at the CT scan room.

The nurse rolled Kevin in as he was greeted by the radiographer behind a thick pane of glass. "Good morning, Mr. Garner, we just need a quick look inside your head. All you need to do is lie down on the table and stay as still as possible. The machine will do the rest." A mechanical ring surrounded one end of the platform Kevin was instructed to rest on, so he stretched out and adjusted into a comfortable position. Kevin took one more look at Katie before laying his head back on the cold surface.

"Okay, now remain calm and remember to keep very still. The ring around your head will rotate while performing the scan," the voice said over an intercom. A quiet whirring sound began to **woosh** in and out, and it reminded him of a white noise he used to fall asleep with. Now Kevin had an uninterrupted twenty minutes to reflect on everything that had transpired in the past week, seemingly within his own mind. He remembered the sinkhole but only bits and pieces. The dreams of the beach at night and the one with the Deer at the campfire were coming to mind, which was strange because he would have normally forgotten dreams like that the next morning. The forest was still a relatively fresh memory, but it felt just like the dreams he used to have when he was younger. Not quite as scripted as a typical dream, but much more real. It was a regular thing to have three or four vivid brain journeys a night when Kevin was a teenager, but about once a week, he became completely self-aware in one of them. Whether it was a TV sitcom-like vision, third person narration of somebody else's life, or a first person nightmare, he ended up with complete control of the outcome. Lucid dreams he had been told they're called.

A few minutes later, he got an, "Okay! You're all set," from the radiologist and the CT machine slowed to a halt.

Nurse Johanna said, "Now for the fun part." Kevin saddled up in his big wheel and was escorted a few doors down on the left. Dr. Seigr was already in the room with another nurse preparing medical instruments and what looked like an operating table. A twinge curled around in his guts because he knew what was about to happen.

Without asking any questions, Kevin stood from his chair and approached the table saying, "Let's just get this over with, shall we?"

The doctor instructed Kevin to lie on his side, so he did. The nurse parted his gown and a cold sensation in the middle of his back was startling, but it was only the rubbing alcohol used to sanitize the skin. The quick pinch of an anesthetic needle, and he couldn't feel a thing. Katie had elected to stay in the hall, and Kevin didn't blame her one bit. "This is going to feel less than desirable," the doctor said as he prepared a much larger needle from behind.

Kevin sarcastically replied with, "Hardy-har, what a funny—" but the rest of his sentence was stolen from him. In an instant, he was no longer himself, but a shadow on the ceiling watching a time-lapse of a patient receiving a spinal tap. Like a pin prick of a water balloon in slow motion, the needle retracted from his flesh to reveal the outline of a human silhouette of water lying on the table. Kevin watched in silent awe as this third person horror unfolded before his eyes. The contents of his mind, body, and spirit spilled over the edges of that table, and his shadow was snatched out of the room from above. Kevin drifted farther and farther away from himself until his shadow melded with the void that had been there all along, ending in total darkness.

Chapter 4
The Rabbit Hole

Down the path, no end in sight,
A creature lurks with web spun tight.

Kevin's fingers grasped at the fallen bed of leaves, and his limbs finished a well-rested stretch. A long, drawn-out yawn echoed through the trees around him. His eyes opened peacefully, as if awakening from a much-needed Sunday afternoon nap. The kind his grandmother's cooking induced after plate number three. Birds were chirping, and a pair of energetic squirrels rustled about in the leaves nearby. Kevin was in the forest once more; the haunting moan and flow of breeze confirmed it. As he raised his head, the glow of the sun shone down through the lush, green canopy, illuminating the path and fallen log he had seen in his dream. Only this time, the mysterious Deer had returned, standing much closer than the first time they met. Similarly as before, and without making a sound, it turned to leap over the log in a single bound, disappearing farther into the forest.

The pouches and gear Kevin had acquired were still laying in the path where he had been violently thrashed for killing a spider. It was at this point he realized this probably wasn't a dream, but what was it? *Am I time traveling? Or teleporting to another world?* Kevin thought, as he tightened the straps on his new backpack – the one brought to him by a magical ram and filled with wild blueberries. The thoughts made him chuckle. Kevin could either continue to rack his brain, stressing about whether or not his sanity would last, or he could surrender to it and allow this journey to transform him. It would most certainly be easier, and after all, he was a man that believed everything happens for a reason. Kevin looked farther down the path in front of him, and he thought, *Let's see how far this rabbit hole goes.*

A subtle grin replaced the neutral expression on his face. He never expected to be thrust into a scenario like the one at hand, and embracing it was even more far-fetched of a thought, but that's exactly what was going to happen. Kevin clenched his fists and moved toward the log to perform a less-than-graceful vault over the giant tree blocking his path. His feet landed squarely on the other side, but not on the beaten dirt path he had been following all along; instead, he encountered a series of small, square stones of different sizes laid out like a cobblestone road. They were the first man-made features he had come across thus far and clearly the only way forward. The brush and branches had become too dense surrounding the path to try and waver from it, and it also didn't seem like a great idea to begin with. If that spider was an example of the less than desirable wildlife, then he wouldn't be taking any unnecessary detours.

Step by step, the scenery didn't change very much besides a low hanging branch to avoid or a root crossing the path to step over. Every foot forward felt like a foot farther from his destination. Kevin didn't even know what the destination was, but that Deer seemed like it might be able to lead him to the answers he was looking for. The ram gave him something, surely the Deer would point him in the direction of the nearest metaphorical rocket ship so he could fly back to reality. If he wasn't dead, and it wasn't a dream, then he must be a lunatic traveling through time and space. Objectively, it didn't sound like a bad gig; it had to beat the daily grind of a blue-collar nine-to-five. Another grin shined through as his thoughts wandered.

The hypnotic pattern of left foot, right foot had Kevin's eyes fixed on the ground as he advanced when—**BAM!** He stepped face-first into a weathered totem of cobblestones, stacked seven feet high in the middle of the path. Luckily, he hadn't reached Mach speed, so he didn't break his nose, but it sure did bruise his ego, even though no one was watching. The column of rubble was covered in moss that had settled in the joints and cracks, and a smoother stone layer made from what looked like granite had been placed about eye-level. The granite was slightly darker in color and appeared to have a faded inscription. He leaned in to get a closer look, removing excess moss, but he still couldn't read it.

Then Kevin remembered he had a seemingly endless supply of water, so he uncorked his leather canteen and poured a generous amount over the words in the stone, scrubbing vigorously and re-rinsing. After a few minutes of work, he could finally make out the message, and of course, it didn't make any sense:

A man with no path, has no name,
He disregards life, and lives in shame,
Lack of respect, he will soon blame,
Or return to the ashes from whence he came.

Kevin's eyes widened, and a lump in his throat began to form once the full message registered. "Is this for me? What the hell does that mean?" he said aloud, scratching his head. The message was ominous and very off-putting. Kevin read it over and over, feeling worse every time he finished the line: *Or return to the ashes from whence he came.* Five minutes passed, and he realized it wasn't accomplishing anything idling around, staring at the riddle. At this point, it was ingrained in his memory, so Kevin stepped past the stones and continued the journey.

The cobbled path had disappeared under a layer of dried silt and mud, probably from a heavy rain. Time went on with each step, as a feeling of frustration arose and distilled into desperation. It was beginning to feel like he had made a terrible mistake venturing this far down the path when he noticed something only a few feet ahead. A quivering chill ran down his spine. Blocking Kevin's way through were the striped legs of that same damn monster arachnid. He was seemingly floating in midair, only this time he was bigger – a lot bigger – like a football with legs bigger. Something born out of science fiction and pure horror. Kevin noticed evidence of a massive, semi-transparent web stretching from tree to tree, completely blocking his walkway. Killing the spider wasn't a choice. Last time, some kind of elemental forest spirit broke him over its knee like a toothpick; he wasn't making that mistake again. His only other options were to tear down the web or turn back. As badly as he wanted to, turning back just didn't make sense, so Kevin picked up the nearest stick that had a reasonable length to it and slowly approached the heavily defended web.

Once within swinging distance, the football-sized hellspawn tensed up and tightened its appendages into a guarded stance. Kevin's trembling hands extended the stick toward the top left corner of the creature's web. He closed his eyes and delivered a swift samurai chop. Not only did he fail to break the web, but it was so sticky, the tree branch slipped out of his grasp and became permanently entangled in the impenetrable net of glue. The web danced back and forth as big daddy furry legs walked across to claim Kevin's sword as a trophy of victory. He earned it, because despite Kevin's best effort, his castle was still standing. *So much for that plan,* Kevin thought as he took a step back. He contemplated his next move while staring down his adversary. "You look pissed," Kevin said to the spider jokingly.

He couldn't help but notice the subtle beauty in the web the spider had created, including the hundreds of threads intricately tied off, connecting ten inner rings that were evenly spaced apart. It was geometrically perfect, not to mention its silvery reflection, due to a few dim sun rays shining down just behind it. You would think it was woven of glass and metal, and it might as well have been, given the strength. It wasn't clear to Kevin if it was his defeat or the beauty of the web, but he had a newfound appreciation for big daddy furry legs.

"I'm sorry I killed you, okay? For the record, I was only retaliating for an invasion of personal space, but I do like your web, buddy, you did a good job on it," he said. After a moment, the spider calmly began moving back to the right side of the silver net and severing the joints he had connected to the trees. One by one, back and forth, he worked his way lower until the web was completely taken down to the ground. Then he dragged the web through the dirt, keeping it taut so the strands wouldn't get bundled up. The fine silt collected on the wire-like strands until every inch was covered. *That's it?* Kevin thought. *Did you ruin your web because I gave you a compliment?* The spider untangled the stick and left the dusty web on the ground;it gave him one more angry look, then scurried off into the forest.

"Thanks, bud," Kevin said under his breath, staring at the ruined piece of art on the ground. He knelt and picked up part of the web with both hands. It had lost its sticky properties but was still just as strong as ever. No amount of tugging could knock even one joint out of alignment. "I could trap an elephant with this thing," he said with another cheeky grin as he folded up his new net and packed it at the bottom of his bag.

After hiking down the path for another mile or so, Kevin was getting tired, and the humidity was making him very thirsty. An old stump presented itself as a perfect rest stop just to the left of the narrow, wooded pathway. Moss and vines had climbed the bark on either side. He sat down and took a few swigs from his canteen, then a few more. It was still ice cold and he loved it. Taking time to rest and breathe, the words of the stone inscription crossed his mind again: *He disregards life, and lives in shame.* Kevin couldn't help but think there had to be a connection with those words and both of his run-ins with the spider. Could this have been a life lesson being taught? He wasn't sure, but his second encounter with the hairy arachnid was much more pleasant. In the end, he had respect for his enemy, and the spider unexpectedly rewarded Kevin's change of heart with a gift that could probably come in handy.

The first part still didn't make any sense: *A man with no path, has no name.* There was no denying that he was on a path, and ironically, he had two names according to Eric-James… Kevin and Thomas. Kevin's days at work in the beginning of the week felt like years ago, and he worried about waking up on another jobsite in the condition he was in. If he was going in and out of consciousness, then at least the medical tests would help answer what was wrong with him. The sound of a twig snapping drew his attention to the Deer sneaking up on him. There he was again, only a few yards away, but this time his unbroken stare had a message: *You must see with more than eyes.* Kevin didn't hear it, but he felt it from within.

The Deer turned and slowly walked back the way he came, but not too fast to follow, so Kevin stood and said, "Yes, Sensei," with a sarcastic exhale. The Deer led him to a small clearing in the woods with a mighty oak in the center. A mossy, ivy-tangled structure made of hand-cut boards with a small opening in the center rested between two large branches of the tree. It reminded him of the treehouse his father had built when he was a child. It took all summer to get it finished because he only had Sundays available to work on it, and Kevin was too young to use any power tools. Kevin and his neighborhood friends would gather on a Saturday and play a game they liked to call "sniper," where a flag was tied to the trunk of the tree and one kid had a Red Ryder BB gun in the "tower." Everyone else took turns running forward and taking cover – the sniper couldn't hit you if you were standing still, otherwise they lost, but if they hit everyone else on the move, then the sniper won. Kevin couldn't remember a single time any of them won as the sniper, but peppering your buddies with BB welts was worth losing every time. Kevin noticed a shadowy movement in the window-like opening that made his heart sink, and a sickening realization was setting in. He wasn't looking at a tree house filled with fond childhood memories, it was a hunting stand.

A deafening blast of light and energy came forth from the window in the structure, resounding through the trees. Kevin felt it in his chest. The shockwave sent him to the ground and a ringing in his ears remained after the echo tapered off. Kevin frantically checked himself for blood or wounds to make sure he hadn't been hit. Luckily, he was fine, but the shot found its mark, nonetheless. Still only a few feet away, the Deer he had been following now lay in the dirt, snorting its last breaths, and a part of Kevin was dying with him. The smell of gunpowder was strong in the air as he looked up to see a few ribbons of smoke floating away from the blind. He rushed over and knelt beside the wounded animal.

Kevin's heart was broken, not only because he didn't want to see the beautiful creature in so much pain, but because the only link he had been able to connect to in this place now lay in a pool of blood. Kevin wasn't a hunter, but even he could tell the wound wasn't in the proper spot for a good, clean kill, which meant his guide wasn't going to die anytime soon, but suffer.

"Don't you touch that damn Deer! That's my kill – you hear me, boy?!" The voice was unfamiliar to him, but it was strange enough hearing it in this place because Kevin thought he was alone.

He turned and shouted back, "What the hell is the matter with you?! You could have killed me! Not to mention you're thirty feet away and only managed to put him in pain! You should be ashamed!"

"Ha! I bet you couldn't hit the broadside of a barn from thirty feet! Now step away from my jerky meat!" the man replied.

Kevin lowered his voice and said, "Well, you have two options – you can either put this Deer out of its misery, or you can shoot me, because I'm not going to stand here and watch him suffer."

"Him?! I bet you named him, too! Let me guess… BAMBI! HAHAHA! I ain't wasting another good bullet, boy, he'll be dead soon, just watch." Ignoring the comment, Kevin turned back to the helpless animal, and with sadness filling his heart to the rim, pulled his knife from its sheath.

The voice shouted again, "Don't you do it, boy! I'll put a hole in you, too!" Kevin rested the tip of the blade on the torso, just behind the elbow, and made eye contact with the creature one last time.

"NO! STOP!" the voice shouted before Kevin sunk the knife up to the hilt. The breathing stopped and so did the pain.

"I'm sorry, my friend," he whispered. Relief took the place of sadness as he rose to his feet and turned to address the hunter, "Two times the coward, I see."

"You're lucky you called my bluff; I'm out of bullets, but any other day and you'd be lying there next to your buddy," the man said in a bragging way.

"First of all, what kind of a hunter only carries one bullet AND has terrible aim? You need to at least practice if you're going to be cocky, and second, how did you even get here? Do you even know what's going on?" said Kevin.

"First of all," the man said in a mockingly cartoonish voice, "You startled me and threw off my shot. That Deer is normally alone, so I wasn't expecting to see anybody else out here. Second, I only ever have one round when I wake up here."

Kevin paused before his reply. Although this man hadn't been pleasant, he might hold the answers he was looking for. "So... you're saying you woke up here too, and you've shot that Deer before?"

"Buddy, I've shot that Deer more times than I can even remember, and I wake up in this prison every other day. This is my forest. The other half of the time is kind of like living in a fuzzy TV. Sounds are dull, my vision is blurry, there are people around me, but they can't hear me when I speak. Ultimately, I'm just as trapped there as I am here. The sun goes down all the same and eventually I fall asleep; when I wake up, I'm somewhere else," the man answered.

YOUR forest?! This is MY journey! Kevin thought to himself. How could any of that be true? Was this crazy hunter pulling his leg? Or was he really stuck in some kind of time loop like he described. *What a miserable existence – for him and for the Deer*, he thought. The structure didn't seem to have any ladder or rope to get up or down with. "Okay, I'm a bit confused. I've only woken up here twice – the first time didn't go so well, and the second time I woke up where I left off. How long have you been doing this? What's your name?" Kevin asked as the figure got closer to the window in the blind. He could make out a forty-something year old man with a bald head and a scruffy chin. He was wearing a worn-out plaid shirt with a red bandana tied around his neck.

"The name's Jacob; it's been this way for decades at least. You're the first person I've ever seen come through here. What's yours?" he asked as he leaned on the sill of his window with crossed arms.

Decades?! Kevin thought to himself. *Could I end up stuck here that long? What got Jacob stuck this way in the first place?* Jacob telling Kevin that the Deer comes back over and over calmed him down a little, but he was still a bit raw from watching it die.

"It's Kevin, though I'm not sure if that's true anymore, could be Thomas... So, you just keep shooting the same Deer over and over? Have you ever considered letting him live? That Deer was pretty much the only reason I found you, and you shot it right in front of me."

Jacob rubbed his forehead as if annoyed and said, "It's in my blood, son, and it's not like I have much else to do up here, and I couldn't have cared less if you found me or not. I've gotten really good at being alone."

"Have you ever tried climbing down? There's a beach two or three miles down that path. I would think working on your tan would be better than staying up there," Kevin replied.

"I hate the beach, and I've tried climbing down, but there's nothing to hold on to but this window ledge. I lose my grip every time, and when I hit the ground, I wake up in TV Land." His answer was less than comforting; Kevin didn't want to find out what TV Land was like. He almost didn't want to ask his next question, but even though Jacob was creating more questions than answers, he was forthcoming with info that might come in handy.

"You... you mentioned you wake up with one bullet... have you ever —"

Jacob cut him off before he could finish. "I have. Same result. It just spits me back into that aggravating place, and I rather like it here nowadays. It's peaceful."

"If I can help you get down, will you come with me? It seems like there's a lot more to this place than just the forest, and you're the only person I've seen here as well. Maybe we can help each other," Kevin asked.

"Kevin, I've been here a long time. I've come to terms with the forest and my condition. I'm not sure what you think we could do about it, but if you can actually manage to get me down, I'll go with you," he responded.

"Give me a minute and we'll find out," Kevin said as he started examining the surroundings for anything that might be of use. He started walking along the tree line, looking for a large branch or a vine long enough to reach the tree stand.

"What is it that you think you need help with, boy?" Jacob asked with a sarcastic tone.

"Well, for starters, you're gonna help me bury this Deer," Kevin said in an equal manner.

"The hell I will! I've killed that Deer over a thousand times, and not once have I been able to make a tasty chewy batch of jerky. I've fantasized about frying homemade venison sausage with a few quail eggs over a campfire ever since I first laid eyes on that big bastard. Don't get me started on the antlers, it's the biggest rack I've ever seen!" he responded. Kevin could tell Jacob was drooling at this point, and he had to admit he was feeling a bit peckish himself.

Out of the corner of his eye, Kevin noticed a shiny glint from underneath a pile of leaves that a rogue beam of sunlight was illuminating. He gently brushed the leaves away, hoping not to disturb any sleeping critters, like another eight-legged beast. Once he had uncovered the object, he stood and, behold, there in front of him lay the same aluminum ladder he had fallen from a week ago. With a chuckle in his words, Kevin said aloud, "Oh good, it followed me again."

"What?! What followed you again? I'm still out of bullets!" Jacob exclaimed with a concerned layer to his voice.

"It's a ladder," Kevin said. He didn't bother telling him that it had tried to kill him a week prior.

"What?! You're telling me I've been stuck up here for years, and there's been a ladder lying on the ground this whole time?!" he shouted again. It looked like it had been buried for a very long time.

"I'm afraid so, Jacob. See? Something's telling me I was supposed to find you out here," Kevin answered. He lifted the ladder, tapping one end against a tree a few times to shake off the rest of the leaves, walked over to the window side of Jacob's prison, and extended a few rungs so it would reach.

"Well, I'll be damned, let me grab my stuff real quick and I'll climb down," Jacob said as he disappeared from the window. Kevin braced his feet at the bottom of the ladder to add support for Jacob's descent and looked over at the Deer again.

Frustration was still brewing within him, but it sounded like there was a chance he would see him again. Kevin still wasn't sure about this Jacob fellow, but he was the best shot he had at figuring out where he was and how to escape. "Okay, I'm coming down," Jacob said as he climbed out the window and mounted the top of the ladder. He was wearing a pair of worn-out khaki-colored overalls and a red flannel shirt. He had a backpack on that seemed to be filled to the brim with what appeared to be camping gear and a scoped hunting rifle draped over his right shoulder.

The little bit of light in the clearing was starting to dim, indicating that the sun was beginning to go down like Jacob had described. Kevin spoke, "You seem to be dressed fairly warm for this weather; does it get cold here at night?" Before he could answer, Jacob lost his footing same as Kevin did and torpedoed down the ladder, boots first. His forehead bounced off a rung halfway down, throwing him off the track of the ladder and into midair. In the blink of an eye, the rubber heel of a boot collided with Kevin's shoulder, thrusting him backwards and off balance. The back of his head struck a tree root protruding from the ground. A cursed ladder was the last thing he saw before a black halo reduced his vision into a bright little dot surrounded by darkness, like an old-fashioned television turning off for the last time.

Chapter 5
Asylum

Open your eyes, follow the rules,
Take the pill, mimic the fools.

Only one eye opened. Kevin couldn't move. All he could see was a red and black tiled pathway leading into a brightly lit zebra-striped opening. He could hear muffled voices all around him – some laughing, some crying. A scratchy vinyl recording of "You Are My Sunshine" was overlapping everything else in the room. Pain was radiating from his right cheek. It was wet, and he still couldn't open his right eye. *Oh no!* He thought to himself, *I've lost an eye, and now I'm trapped in TV Land!*

After a few minutes, Kevin felt circulation returning to his arms and legs. Then the nausea set in. As he gained his bearings, he could tell his hands were in his lap and he was hunched over. With all his might, he forced himself to sit upright and lifted his head from the cold wet surface, only to be smacked with a disorienting vertigo. It reminded Kevin of his younger days, when he would drink too much and get the "spins." His stomach took control, and he had no choice but to keel over and vomit, but nothing came up. It felt like he hadn't eaten in days. Just like his first trip to the plateau. As his vision began to clear up, he kept his head as still as possible to avoid the vertigo; the nausea began to subside.

Kevin's right eye slowly opened. He took note of his surroundings. He was wearing a white T-shirt and a flannel robe with pinstripe pajama bottoms. The red and black tiles were a checkerboard, placed on a small table that he had been drooling on, and the bright zebra pattern was a window covered in iron bars. There was a deep indentation on his right cheek from a checker piece and must have been why it was so sore. Sitting across from him was an old man with a blank stare on his face. It was Jacob! He could tell by his bald head, and he was still wearing the red bandana around his neck. Only he had aged by forty years or more, and so had Kevin. Liver spots and wrinkles covered his hands, and the voices he heard were coming from other elderly people engaged in random activities like sewing or drawing with crayons.

Kevin turned to the old man and said, "Hey… Jacob, it's me, Kevin! Can you hear me? We're in some sort of psychiatric ward. Is this the other place you go besides the forest?" He prayed the answer would be no, but then again, he wasn't sure what the alternative could possibly be.

Jacob locked his thousand-yard stare on Kevin and said, "King me? King me! King me, King me, King me, King me, KING ME!!!" then returned to his catatonic state.

What the hell? Kevin thought. Drool was still dripping from his chin when the red checker piece that was stuck to his cheek fell, bounced off the little table, and rolled across the floor. The Jacob he had met in the forest was long gone, and now he was trapped in Jacob's own personal hell.

Kevin looked around once more and noticed a handful of caregivers interacting with the patients, one was an older nurse with silvery, peppered hair. Another was a young man pacing back and forth keeping an eye on everyone and commenting on the beautiful macaroni art. The third caregiver in the room was a younger woman who had bright red hair and dark green eyes playing cards with one of the patients. She was pretty, but the longer Kevin looked at her, the deeper an unsettling feeling sank in. He had met her before, but from where? Why was his gut telling him to avoid her at all costs? Last, a very large security guard was standing at the end of the room guarding a door. It had a sign hanging above it that read *STAFF ONLY.* There was one other door to the right of the barred window, and from where he was sitting, it looked like it led into a courtyard.

Kevin turned back to Jacob and was startled by the presence of the older nurse standing next to him, looking down with eyes open wide. The nurse had black nail polish, which was strange to see on an older lady. She must have been in her seventies. A black rose brooch was pinned to her uniform just below the left side of the collar, and on the right, a name tag that read *Nurse Dahlia,* which was fitting due to her Rouge Noir style. She held an awkward, silent glare for a few seconds before raising the palm of her hand, which held the red checker piece. "You've lost it," she said as she set the piece down on the table and handed Kevin a rag for his face.

"Thank you," he said, wiping the saliva from his cheek and chin. There was another awkward pause before she asked what his name was and if he had just gotten there. "Yes, ma'am, my name is Kevin," was his brief response. Even his voice had aged, with his words coming off soft-spoken and feeble.

"I see," were her last words before turning and walking away to check on other patients. A digital clock on the wall read *6:38PM*, but Kevin's internal clock was telling him it was morning. The two younger caregivers approached each other and words were exchanged that he couldn't make out, then they both approached the restricted doorway and the musclebound enforcer let them through. There must have been twelve to fifteen lost sheep wandering around the rec room, all of which were in comfortable lounging attire like him. Some were sitting completely still, like Jacob, while others were moving around frantically and mumbling to themselves about this and that; however, one patient caught Kevin's eye.

In the far corner of the room sat a young man, maybe thirty years old, looking directly at him, completely devoid of emotion. He seemed so familiar, but Kevin just couldn't place the name. The longer he looked, the deeper the same ominous feeling sank in that he had while looking at the woman with red hair. He was more than twenty feet away from him, but Kevin could tell his eyes were black as night and they were cutting into him like a hot knife through butter. Yet again, Kevin didn't know where he was or how he got there, but one thing was certain, this guy did not approve of his presence whatsoever.

He had only been conscious in this place for a few minutes and couldn't wait to get out. Kevin told himself that all he needed to do was go to sleep and he would be back in the forest or maybe even back in the hospital with his wife. This all according to Jacob, the lunatic sitting across from him. Kevin slowly stood from his chair, and the movement sent aching pains down his back and legs. His joints were stiff and his muscles had withered. Kevin was an old man and the path he perceived to be showing the way home was now hidden from him. He had learned the rules of the forest through trial and error, but this was a whole new ball game, along with its own set of rules to learn.

Once erect, Kevin faced the window to get a better look at the courtyard. To his astonishment, there, standing in the middle of the courtyard, with no way in or out, stood the magnificent Deer that Jacob had shot minutes before. He was pilfering a huge tomato growing in a raised flower bed. "Jacob, look! Do you see that?! He's alive!" Kevin shouted at him as he turned to see.

Jacob cut a cheeky grin and raised his right arm, formed a finger gun with his hand, pointed at the Deer, and whispered, "Bang…"

"Very funny," Kevin said to him with a raised eyebrow. When he looked back, his antlered companion was staring right at him, peering into his soul once more with a new message: *In order to see, you must set yourself free,* was etched into the depths of his mind.

Kevin couldn't have been happier. It meant that there was still hope, and although he didn't exactly know what that hope was, at least the clues were still coming to him. Everyone turned to see the two caregivers return to the room with a cart carrying containers of food and a tray full of little cups. Kevin rubbed his eyes and returned his attention to the courtyard, but the Deer was already gone. "Dinner time!" the redhead shouted as the two caregivers began passing out Styrofoam containers. One by one, the patients were handed a box and two small white cups, like the ones you see at a dentist office for rinsing and spitting. They'd throw one back, then the other without hesitation, but Kevin had seen enough movies to know one held medication and one held water.

There was no way in hell he was going to take any pills in a place he just woke up in. Though Kevin still wasn't sure exactly what was happening to him or where he was, he knew he wasn't crazy. According to a few psychological thrillers he had seen, once you take the pill, that's it, game over. Kevin had to think of something fast. The duo got closer and closer as he began to panic; they were checking under every tongue to make sure the drugs had been swallowed. *C'mon, Kevin, think! Think!* he pleaded with himself. Before he knew it, the two were on top of them, and

Jacob was downing his daily dose of sunshine. Then a lightbulb went off in Kevin's head – eight months ago he had an oral procedure done to remove his wisdom teeth, and the gaping pits left behind in the back of his mouth had healed and sealed up, all but one on the bottom right.

It didn't heal quite right and would catch food morsels from time to time. So, if he could use his tongue and stuff the pill down into his gums, with any luck, they might not be able to tell the difference between a real tooth and a pill. While they were still focused on Jacob and peering into his mouth, Kevin started chewing on a dry corner of his drool rag to soak up as much moisture as possible. He figured a deranged individual chewing on a rag wouldn't seem out of place if he meant to play the part. Now it was Kevin's turn, and his heart was racing. It was now or never, and the best shot he had at maintaining any type of lucidity.

The young man set his box of dinner on the table and the redhead handed Kevin his two cups. First the pill, then the water. With as fluid of a motion as possible, he inserted the pill into the back-right side of his mouth and tossed the water back on the left in order to keep the pill dry. With a theatrical gulp, Kevin looked at the caregiver and opened his mouth, wagging his tongue from left to right then up and down. The plan would have been executed perfectly if it wasn't for nurse Dahlia walking over to inquire about who was going on break first in the morning.

Now there were three of them standing right in front of him, bickering back and forth about who had done more the day before. Kevin thought he was in the clear, but he was starving, and he caught a whiff of meatloaf escaping his dinner box. Salivating was unavoidable, and the capsule with a mind-numbing compound was beginning to melt. The disgusting chemical taste of the capsule was seeping into his mouth, like gargling with dish soap. Kevin had time to read the younger caregivers' name tags. One was Murphy, the other was Tammy. He caught the last few words said, which were, "Well, then who's it gonna be?" Without hesitation, he pointed to the redhead, showing his teeth with a wide smile. "Well, it looks like Kevin has spoken! At least somebody around here has common sense," Tammy said, as the three of them began to walk away, laughing at the ironic comment.

Kevin frantically started grabbing at the mushy gel capsule to remove as much as possible, but it had already fallen apart. He was able to get most of it out with his tongue and by spitting into the rag, but part of it was still there and there was nothing he could do about it. The horrible taste would be a fairly permanent part of the rest of his day as it slowly dissolved and absorbed into his gums. Whatever it was, at least he didn't get the full dose. Kevin leaned in closer to Jacob and asked, "So, all we have to do is go to sleep and we'll get out of here right, Jacob?"

His eyes got wide and seemed as though they were holding back a secret. With a distraught look on his face, he replied, "There is no getting out…" It was troubling, but Kevin couldn't put much stock in anything he said in his condition.

Twenty minutes later, the meatloaf had hit the spot. Almost as good as his grandmother's recipe. Almost. At eight-thirty, it was bedtime, and the caregivers began herding the patients toward the guarded door. Kevin followed in line as the door opened and they marched down a hallway that led to a T-intersection. The wall at the end of the hallway was lined with wide glass windows and looked to be an employee break room. Turning right would lead you down to a dead end door with a sign that read *OFFICE*. They turned left and then turned right down another hall. He was in the back of the line and noticed another sign that read *LINEN CLOSET*. A few more steps and they were ushered through a set of double doors to a room filled with bunk beds.

All the cuckoos nestled and left one bottom bunk vacant for Kevin. By chance, Jacob was lying in the one to the right, but the bunk to the left was occupied by none other than the potential serial killer who was giving him the death stare earlier. He was lying on his side in a curled position, facing Kevin's bunk, and he didn't blink. Kevin could feel his eyes on him as he slowly pulled the covers up to his chest and looked at the slats supporting the bunk above. He was restless and not sure if Charles Manson was going to look away or even go to sleep. Eventually, sleepiness set in as a heavy fog, which was probably the bit of happy pill he had ingested. As the fog got thicker, Kevin relaxed and looked forward to finding the Deer in the forest again to ask a few philosophical questions. Breathing deepened, mouth hung open, his eyes closed.

Screams of horror jumpstarted Kevin's heart in the morning. "No, no, no, NO, NOOOO!" boomed from his right like a loudspeaker. It was Jacob, and he was losing it, frantically running from his bunk.

"Oh my head," Kevin said. Not only did he have what felt like the worst hangover of his life, but they were still trapped in that asylum. Jacob was trying to ram his way through the door when the Goliath security guard burst through and wrapped him up like a python. The caregivers followed in short order and administered a large needle to his backside. The screaming slowed and was followed by miserable groans that eventually came to a halt, along with his squirming. The guard dragged him out of the room as the patients stood and lined up by the door like nothing happened. *Oh, that's not good,* Kevin thought to himself as he stood and took his place as the caboose on the looney train. Nurse Dahlia was standing close by as they began to move, so he asked, "Where are they taking him?"

"The ice tank, that's where they take patients to 'cool off,' so to speak." Her tone indicated that she didn't approve either, and just like that, they were back in the rec room, but now his fellow checkers player was MIA. As breakfast was brought in, along with another dose of medication, Kevin thought of the message the Deer had sent the day before. He was sure that, *In order to see, you must set yourself free,* must hold some philosophical meaning, but he was planning on taking it literally. He was getting out of here one way or another.

Kevin's stomach began to grumble as the smell of biscuits and sausage gravy filled the air while Murphy and Tammy made their rounds like before. He didn't have any problem fooling the two with his disappearing pill trick, which he promptly discarded.

After finishing breakfast, Kevin was laying the foundation of his escape plan when a low tone chimed from the clock and the patients began lining up at the courtyard door like programmed robots. Single file, they made their way into the courtyard and most resumed routine activities. Kevin found a chair with the best view to begin his surveillance. Maybe fifty feet by fifty feet, the courtyard floor was concrete and surrounded by two-story brick walls, with windows on the second floor. The only entrance being the door they came through and nothing seemed to stand out, except for an old copper gutter pipe hanging loose from one of the inner corners of the roof. *Hmm… if I can get a rope or something draped over that gutter and tie it off somewhere down below, I might be able to pull myself up onto the roof,* he thought.

Yet again, Kevin was startled by her abrupt presence as nurse Dahlia found a chair next to him and said in a serious tone, "You don't belong here, Kevin," as she stared at the half-eaten tomato still lying next to the raised vegetable garden. He was stunned by the comment and wasn't sure whether to keep his cover or scream *EXACTLY!* She turned and continued, "What I mean is, you're from somewhere else aren't you? A different time, a different life."

Still stunned, he nodded and said nervously, "How do you know that?" She looked back at the tomato and told Kevin something that would follow him for the rest of his life.

"This place isn't real, Kevin, it's all in Jacob's head. The only elements that I know are real are you, me, and Jacob himself. What I'm still trying to figure out is how you got here." Eyes wide and jaw dropped, like a little kid listening to a good adventure story, Kevin faced her and listened intently. "My name is Roxanna Dahlia, and I'm a twenty-six year old grad student working at the Kenneth-Ashan Neurology Research Facility in Colorado. My dissertation includes a theory of using the subconscious to communicate with people who suffer from complete psychosis and other mental conditions. Tell me, have you ever heard of lucid dreaming?"

"I have, actually, I used to lucid dream often when I was younger," he responded.

"Well, I've spent years training myself to do it as often as possible, almost every night. I can start a dream in any location, in any time period, with anyone or anything. I've been able to locate over twenty of our volunteer test subjects within their own minds, as long as they are asleep as well. The only problem is, none of them have ever remembered our interactions when they wake up, so I have no way of proving I'm making the connection in the first place," she explained.

"This sounds nuts…" Kevin said.

"Just listen. Jacob's case is the most severe one I've been looking into. In real life, he is a Vietnam veteran with Alzheimer's disease. He can't verbally communicate anymore, but he's the closest I've come to confirming my research so far, and if I don't come up with concrete evidence soon, the

KAN Research Facility could lose interest in my project and start focusing on the pharmaceutical profits. My PhD will hang in the balance. Somehow, you've entered Jacob's subconscious, potentially in a different way than I have. Every element of this part of Jacob's subconscious is static, meaning nothing ever changes. Not until you showed up, and the way you got here could be the key to proving my theory," she explained.

"So, you're saying I'm not a time traveler or a teleporter?" Kevin asked, and as he said the words, it almost disappointed him in a strange way.

"Precisely," she replied. "Jacob is normally this old in the waking world, but his subconscious has manifested this place for him to dwell while asleep. I suspect to harbor him from the vicious nightmares brought on from his time at war. I'm not totally sure why you and I are this age, perhaps it's an effect of outsiders becoming part of someone else's dream, to make the individual more comfortable with the changes. After all, it's their dream and I can only conclude that means we are forced to go by their rules, whether Jacob is aware of them or not."

Kevin sat in silence for a few seconds, trying his best to absorb everything she was saying. Her explanation of Jacob's case made sense, but it still didn't shine much light on his... He looked back at the tomato before further questioning nurse Dahlia.

"I keep seeing this strange Deer; he seems to be guiding me in some way, but I'm not sure. Can you tell me anything about him?"

She replied, "I've seen him a handful of times here in Jacob's world. The few times he has been coherent enough to speak with, the deer shows up and Jacob gets distracted. By the way he stares and licks his lips, I'd say he must have been a hunter in his younger days, which would explain why the deer keeps showing up in his subconscious." Kevin tried to interject and clarify his concern, but Roxanna was already on to her next point. "Now, Kevin, I'll need some personal info, like full name, address, etc., and with your consent, I can potentially get in contact with you or a loved one in the waking world. Then we can have a much clearer picture of what's going on with you."

"Sure, my name is Kevin Garner, I live at 12… 9… uhhh…" He paused. Why couldn't he remember his own address? The longer he tried to think about who he was, the less sense it made. Kevin began to panic and exclaimed, "I can't remember my address! I can't even remember my wife's name!"

She calmed him down and said, "It's okay, it's okay, this is a common symptom of being submerged for as long as you have. I promise your memory will return. In the meantime, I can start cross-referencing your name. I know a guy that might be willing to violate a few HIPAA laws for dinner and a movie. If you've been to the hospital for a medical condition recently, I'll be able to find you."

"I have, or at least I think I have. There's a foggy memory of waking up in a hospital and medical testing to rule out certain conditions, but I'm not even sure if it was real anymore..." he answered.

"Then there's a chance," she said with a smile on her wrinkled face. "Don't lose this, Kevin, you're going to need it—" nurse Dahlia said as she reached into her pocket and concealed a small key ring in her palm, which she then placed into his. Kevin released a deep breath of hope as she silently stood up and walked away. There were a hundred more questions that were burning holes in his brain, but the key ring brought on a calm satisfaction and with it a newfound determination to continue his plot of escape.

A few hours later, it was time for everyone to return to the rec room and eat lunch. Club sandwiches, chips, and a pickle were served with an ice-cold cola. Even though he was trapped in a psych ward, the food was pretty damn good. Kevin spent the afternoon in silence, contemplating possible fail-safes for his plan, until Murphy came through the secured door guiding a drooling Jacob back to their checkers table. His eyes were fixed on the floor and the effects of the sedative he had received in the morning were still very much present in his bloodstream.

Kevin told him, "I'm getting out of here tonight, Jacob. I've got a plan. Nurse Dahlia gave me a set of keys, and if I can get a few bed sheets from the linen closet, I think I can climb up to the roof from the gutter and lower myself down the other side. I want you to come with me." Jacob looked up at him as if to answer, then looked out the window toward the gutter he was speaking of. A gentle nod of Jacob's head was all he needed. Keven knew he was on board.

They had begun to play a slow-paced game of checkers when nurse Dahlia walked over with a bit of useful information. "The security guard's name is Johnny, and today is his birthday. I've offered to bake him a cake that the staff and patients will share after dinner. I suggest you two avoid eating it if you want to be able to walk out of here tonight. I'll be back later," she said with a wink, then headed out the door guarded by Johnny.

Kevin looked at Jacob and said, "How's that for poetic justice? She's gonna drug the staff for us tonight! Looks like ole Johnny's gonna get a taste of his own medicine." A familiar grin spread across Jacob's face.

A few games of checkers later, and the sun started going down. The same low tone chime came from the clock on the wall, and it was time for dinner. The caregivers disappeared for a moment before returning with another cart full of food, but this time the smell was horrible, like rotten garbage. Brussels sprouts and chicken livers. If they were fried, Kevin might have been able to handle it, but he had to turn down the meal, despite the rest of them being delicious. Jacob had finished scarfing down the gruel when nurse Dahlia finally came back with a large platter carrying a homemade birthday cake. *Right on time,* he thought as she began to sing "Happy Birthday" for Johnny. Caregivers Murphy and Tammy began preparing plates of cake to pass around, and before long, everyone was stuffing their faces with sunshine-laced cake, all except nurse Dahlia, Jacob, and Kevin. What he thought was going to be a daunting task – masterminding a great escape – was turning out to quite literally be a piece of cake.

Nurse Dahlia returned and mentioned, "I would wait at least an hour after bedtime to make sure the staff are good and under. They normally hang around the break room until about ten before heading to their own quarters, but I suspect the lot of them won't make it that far – after all, the secret ingredient in the cake is a whole bottle of Clonazepam. Johnny is the biggest, so once he goes down, you're in the clear."

"Hold on, if we leave, how are you going to be able to find us again?" Kevin asked.

"Don't worry, I've spent enough time with you and learned enough about you. I'll be able to find you and Jacob, wherever this path takes you, although you might not hear from me for a while. I have research to do and a Kevin Garner to find. Look after each other for me. Till we meet again." Nurse Dahlia turned and exited the way she came.

It was about eight-thirty now, and even Johnny was yawning and showing signs of lethargy. Murphy was already snoring when the clock chimed its final time for the evening, signaling to the birdies it was time for bed. Single file down the hall they marched toward the bunks, and the staff slithered into the break room on cue. The keys were still in Kevin's robe pocket and had to be carefully placed under his pillow before crawling into bed. He hung up his robe on a bedpost and laid his head down. "Get some rest, I'll wake you up," he said to Jacob, who was wide awake. Kevin could tell he was just as excited as he was. He gave Kevin a nod, rolled on his side and closed his eyes. He peered to his left and noticed that even the neighborhood nightmare was passed out like a fat kid in a tryptophan coma on Thanksgiving.

Now all Kevin had to do was sneak down the hall, tie a few bed sheets together from the linen closet, unlock a few doors, and climb to freedom. He counted every second of every minute that passed until he was sure it was at least ten. Clenching the key ring in his hand so it wouldn't make any noise, Kevin sat up and nudged Jacob awake. "It's time," he whispered, and the two started making their way to the bunk room door.

The set of double doors were dead bolted from the outside and had keyholes on the inside, but one of the keys nurse Dahlia gifted him was labeled *BUNKS*. As quietly as possible, he inserted the key and turned it until they heard a **click**. The door slowly swung open and the first thing he saw was the break room lights and Big Johnny's bald head bobbing up and down through the break room window. "Get down," Kevin whispered to Jacob as fast as he could. The security guard was still nodding off, watching some mindless, late-night sitcom.

They sat in silence for a few more minutes until Johnny's chin tucked to his chest and stayed there. The linen closet was only a few feet away, but for good measure they ducked down and moved slowly to not create any extra noise. Another key on the ring read *LINEN* and unlocked the closet door, revealing a shelf full of fresh clean bed sheets. "Here, hold these," Kevin said as he shoved six or seven of them into Jacob's arms. He looked down at the key ring once more. The last key had a label that read *REC*, so they shuffled down the hall to the familiar door where Johnny was always posted. Kevin unlocked the door and they were through, headed for the courtyard door. A red checker piece was lying on the floor a few feet in front of the door, so he decided to pick it up as a memento, a trophy of sorts for making it this far.

"King me," Jacob said.

"King me, indeed!" Kevin replied. He looked through the key ring and realized they had used all of the keys, and none of them had a label for the courtyard. His heart sank. *Have we really come this far, just to be stopped by one damn door?* Kevin thought to himself in frustration. With his head hung low, he tried to think. Jacob maneuvered in front of him, dropped the bundle of sheets in his arms, grasped the handle, and the door gently swung open.

"King me," Jacob said again.

Thank God it was already unlocked, and thank God for Jacob's common sense, which apparently Kevin had none of at the moment. When the door opened, a small, folded piece of cardboard fell to the floor – it had been wedged between the frame and latch. The lack of lighting made it hard to see, but when he picked it up, Kevin realized it had been written on. The message read:

I bet you thought you weren't going to be able to eat your cake too.

Take care of yourselves, I'll see you soon.

R

If it wasn't for nurse Dahlia, none of his plans would have been possible. Kevin owed her big time, and as far as he was concerned, anything she needed for her research she could have. They headed into the courtyard, and Jacob wedged a folding chair underneath the handle. Kevin began unfolding the sheets and tying corners together with double knots. *SHIT!* he thought to himself. "Jacob, look for something we can use as a weight and tie to one end. We won't be able to get these bed sheets very high without one," Kevin said as he continued to construct their linen ladder of freedom. He hadn't even considered how they would get the bed sheets up and over the gutter.

Suddenly, a blood curdling shriek echoed through the courtyard from inside the rec room. There at the window, to their dismay, stood the nightmarish patient with jet black eyes. His teeth gnashed, as foam dripped from his chin. "Jacob, hurry!" Kevin shouted, as the creature of a man began beating and bashing his way through the blocked door. Jacob ran over, carrying an armful of cucumbers, stolen from the garden. *They're gonna have to do,* he thought, while bundling them into one end and tying it off like a pouch. "We've got one shot at this!" Kevin shouted as a look of terror crossed

Jacob's face. The banging got louder and louder as the bricks around the frame began to crack and dents formed in the steel door. Swinging the bundle of produce around and around, Kevin aimed for the bent gutter and hoped for the best. The bed sheets left his hand, and their hopes of freedom went flying through the air.

"KING ME!!!" Jacob shouted as the cucumber counterweight dangled to the ground. The bed sheets were draped over the gutter as good as they were going to get. Kevin's hands were shaking as he tied one end to an old brass sprinkler tap protruding from the wall. A few test tugs, and he placed his feet on the wall, allowing the bed sheets to support his full weight. A loud **CRASH** erupted from behind that sounded like a car being ripped apart. They looked back and saw a cloud of smoke clearing around an open cavity in the brick wall where the steel door once hung on its hinges. Surrounded by dust and rubble, the panting psychopath approached with bloodied fists. Jacob looked back at Kevin and shouted, "CLIMB!" as he charged toward the ominous creature that seemed to be possessed by something otherworldly.

Kevin started climbing as fast as he could, not looking back, even though Jacob's haunting screams of agony tore through his heart as he grappled with the dark being. "CLIMB! CLIMB! CLIMB!" is the last

he heard from Jacob as the copper gutter pipe came into arm's reach. Despite the frailty of this older form of himself, the adrenaline pushed Kevin to his limits. As he pulled himself onto the shingled roof, he caught a brief glimpse of Jacob, bear-hugging the creature, holding it in place with all his might. For an old, medicated psych patient, he was doing a good job. A quick flash of dark light burst from the demon's chest with a deafening blast of sound that sent Jacob through the air and into the brick wall behind him with a thud that shook the building.

"NO!!!" Kevin shouted, then the beast turned its gaze on him and let out another ravenous roar, before charging on all fours toward the bed sheet ladder. Kevin took off, running to the other end of the roof screaming, "Oh God! Oh God! Oh God!" He made it over the peak, when another loud crash came from behind him that toppled his footing and sent him sliding uncontrollably toward a two-story fall. The beast had vaulted itself thirty feet into the air to close in on its prey in a matter of seconds. Kevin was sliding feet first to his doom. He looked back to see an upside down, wolf-like humanoid galloping across the shingles only a few yards back.

The edge of the roof came and went in an instant. Sound and the speed of the moment went away from him. Time slowed as gravity sent Kevin sailing into a dark abyss. His fear of the chase was gone, along with any other feeling, and what he expected to be a parking lot or a street intersection was pure nothingness. Farther and farther he drifted from the roof's edge, where the demon chose not to follow. A heaviness pulled at Kevin's eyelids, and they slowly closed as his weightless body dissipated into ash.

Chapter 6
Down the Drain

Life in the bottle, drop by drop,
Break the cycle, or the pain won't stop.

Kevin was jarred awake by the blaring sound of an eighteen-wheeler air horn on the street somewhere close by. Another splitting headache to greet him in a new place, along with nausea and body aches. He couldn't completely open his eyes at first, a light shining through a doorway across the room made it difficult. A ceiling fan with a bent blade spun around on the low setting, not doing much in the way of airflow. It was hot, like eighty-five degrees indoors hot, and he was drenched in sweat. Out of all the places his mind had taken him thus far, this was the most unpleasant. Kevin took a moment to look around the room. It was a studio apartment, and one he didn't recognize, with trash and empty pizza boxes strewn about. A few pieces of beat-up furniture, including an old worn-out couch that looked familiar, were lining the walls of a cramped, living room setting.

After a few moments he stretched out, and his left arm bumped into the wall at elbow length. Kevin had been sleeping on a very small cot, and his feet knocked over a cluster of empty beer bottles when he swung his legs over the edge to sit upright. "What the..." he said aloud. The thirst he had was almost unbearable, and then the thought of the ice-cold leather canteen crossed his mind. *Damn, what I wouldn't give for a few swigs of that spring water,* Kevin thought to himself. He was back to reality it would seem, but not nearly the reality he hoped for. The slow drip of a leaky faucet caught his attention, and he stood up to make his way toward the source. The kitchenette of this apartment was disgusting; including a pile of dishes in the sink, a moldy loaf of bread that looked like it hadn't moved in years, and a steady trail of ants leading directly into the refrigerator that was left ajar.

The sink faucet handle almost didn't move at first, seemingly rusted into the closed position, but with a bit of persuasive effort, it opened enough to allow a weak trickle of questionable water to flow.

With cupped hands, Kevin squeezed past the pile of dishes, and started collecting water to drink, handful after handful. It was lukewarm and tasted like metal, but he didn't care. The stream of water that flowed past the dirty dishes in between gulps created a horrid stench that was coming from the bottom of the sink. After drinking plenty of the rusty water, he realized his thirst still wasn't quenched, but this was a different thirst entirely. An open, half-full bottle of vodka on the counter was staring Kevin down, and the insatiable need to take a drink began to dominate him. He had been living sober for three years, and not once in his recovery did he have a craving like this.

Kevin looked away and broke the chain of thought long enough to start looking for clues as to where he was and what had happened. An old documentary on the war in Vietnam was playing on the TV, with the volume turned all the way down. He walked over to the old couch and sat down with his head in his hands. Stricken with grief, Kevin remembered Jacob giving him time to escape the asylum and that he had left him behind. Jacob gave up his freedom so that he could get away, and it made him sick to his stomach. "And all for what? To wake up in this cesspit, fallen off the wagon?! WHO AM I!" Kevin shouted at the TV.

The weight of his situation was finally

starting to sink in, and it felt like an all too familiar rock bottom scenario. The glass doorway that let in the blinding light led to a small balcony and was wide open. "No wonder it's so freaking hot in here," Kevin exhaled. He walked over and stepped out to get some fresh air and clear his head. Another pile of beer cans and empty bottles stood next to a collapsible lawn chair with a small terra cotta pot in the cup holder, filled with cigarette butts. He was in the city, and the streets below were filled with people and cars, making way too much noise for his taste. The headache was getting worse, and the smell of asphalt and sewage drove Kevin back inside in seconds flat. *Where is my wife?* He thought to himself. *Where is Boone?*

There was no evidence to be found of his family ever being there at all, not even a single dog hair. A ripped open envelope and a letter lay on the ground by the door at the far end of the room, leading out of the apartment. Upon retrieving the letter and unfolding it, Kevin took a seat on the couch and realized he recognised the handwriting:

Kevin,

I stopped by a few times last week to check on you, but you didn't come to the door. I hope this letter finds you in good health, but I suspect not. William and I are moving back to Georgia to be closer to family, and Boone is coming with us. I

The letter slipped from his fingertips to the floor, and his knees followed. Breath was scarce, but the tears remained harbored away. A pressure was building in his chest that made it impossible to cry, even though the emotional pain caused his hands to tremble. Kevin's love was gone, and based on the current state of things, she wasn't coming back. Every other mistake he had made in life so far was inconsequential compared to this blunder. *How could I have let this happen?* he thought to himself. *Who is William?! Do I have a son I don't know about? Or does Katie already have a new man?* Neither thought made him feel any better, but he did find solace in remembering her name.

The letter stayed on the floor where he found it, as he stood and frantically started searching the room for evidence of what day it could possibly be. No calendar, no newspaper, not even a cell phone could be found in the filth he was wallowing in. "The news!" Kevin shouted at the TV again. "Where's the remote… where's the damn rem—" he stopped shouting abruptly when a small black triangle with a red button caught his eye, peeking out from under a pizza box. Clenched in a trembling hand, Kevin shuffled his way through a plethora of public programming channels. Jewelry sales, resort advertisements, investment opportunities, etc., until finally – a news station delivering its daily guess at what the weather was going to do.

"A beautiful day today, here in Richmond, Virginia! Eighty-three degrees and sunny now, with a high of eighty-five and a chance of a few passing clouds this evening…" uttered the pinstripe puppet.

"Lies… it's a hundred degrees out there," Kevin mumbled, then he saw it – in the bottom left corner of the screen – the date he was looking for: *JULY 2, 2020.*

"I've… I've lost over two years…" he said in a deflated voice. How could it have been possible? First an afternoon, then four days, and now two years were completely gone from his memory. It was no wonder he was in such shambles, and his wife had moved on and found someone to treat her better. In silence, the feeling sank in. Worthlessness and despair were planting their roots in his stomach, and it wasn't long before those thoughts started shedding light on his true and final desire. Kevin's life was pointless now; not only had he lost everything, but he was only going to lose more, over and over. Kevin wished he could just press a button and jump to the plateau with the Deer and live out the rest of his years in peace. He hadn't even gotten the chance to check out that beautiful beach, but that place had a very distinct mission for him, and he clearly failed.

Kevin was twenty-six years old when he made the choice to finally give up alcohol, and his sobriety lasted three years before he woke up in this shithole. Now he had lost everything he held dear and the will to live was fading fast. He rubbed his eyes with the palms of his hands, then looked up to catch a glimpse of what looked like a wispy, black smoke seeping over the edge of the cheap kitchenette countertop. Kevin's thought process was broken, and he sprang into action. He was indeed ready for his life to end, but he knew for sure he didn't want to burn to death in a studio inferno. Stumbling and scrambling his way to the source of the smoke, he discovered nothing. Not the smoke, nor the smell of anything burning. He checked all the stove burners and did a quick sweep for any soot or ash, but nothing.

Heart racing, Kevin said to himself, *Must have been my imagination or an illusion of some sort.*

Deep down he knew he was just losing his mind, and there was enough to deal with at the moment to be worried about imaginary fire. The bottle of vodka on the counter landed directly in his sights once more, and its gaze sank its claws into him. It was at that moment that Kevin decided he was done running, done fighting. Kevin was just plain done. Kevin throttled the neck of the bottle and brought the poison to his lips. He squeezed with all his might, halfway hoping that the glass would shatter and fall to the floor, but it didn't. The first few sips carried a familiar burn that he craved, which led to a few more that went down easier and easier. Four or five shots in, a tingling set into his fingertips, and a lightheaded warmth that he remembered all too well was priming the rest of his evening alone.

Kevin's personal problem with alcohol was not that he couldn't resist the drink, but that it was an all-powerful medication that solved everything that ailed him. If he was depressed, he would drink. If he was angry, he would drink. Worst of all, even in happiness, he would drink. So now, like before, his problems were washing away with every gulp of fire. Once the bottle was empty, the distraught feeling set in that the medicine was gone and his euphoria would eventually go away. Rummaging like a fiend, each cabinet door remained open as he searched for another bottle. The cabinets were empty, but upon peering into the refrigerator for the first time, he could breathe easy. A chilled bottle of white rum stood next to a half-empty case of beers.

Kevin's problems were over, at least that's what he would subliminally tell himself every time he got his hands on enough alcohol to black out. Before long, an hour had passed, and the twelve beers were gone. The creative juices were flowing, and the fun loving drunk that everyone loved to see at the party was back. The drink gave him the liquid courage and confidence that he lacked in sobriety, so naturally, it was hard to put down in social settings. The sun was going down now and Kevin had been stumbling around, laughing at memories as they passed by and singing half the words to songs he used to know. Back and forth he paced, when the sorrowful regret finally caught up with him.

It finally sunk in, as Kevin swayed and stumbled, that his life was over. And there was no desire to start anew. He fought back the all too sobering tears with the intention of finishing the bottle in the fridge. He needed more because he could still feel pain, and as long as he kept drinking, everything would be okay. Kevin stomped into the kitchen like an off-balance, pouting toddler to retrieve the chilled rum. On the way back to the couch, he tripped over the garbage on the floor and fell forward. Dropping the bottle wasn't going to happen. His one free hand was sliced deep on the jagged edge of an open tin can as he tried to brace his fall. Kevin hissed through his teeth in pain and hurried into the bathroom as blood dripped and stained the carpet along the way.

Water from the faucet burned as it washed over his wound and sent a spiral of blood down the drain. For a moment, he was comforted by a distant memory of Katie nursing one of his carpentry wounds and he thought, *I really wish she was here right now...* Almost in a trance, his mind replayed other fond and happy memories. "What am I doing?" Kevin said aloud. He didn't need to go backward, he needed to be a man and move forward. A glimpse of clarity showed Kevin there was nothing holding him back from fighting to regain everything he had lost, including Katie, his old life, and his own soul. It was an attractive enough concept, to get sober again and be the man he was. However, that didn't make tipping the bottle over the edge of the sink any easier. He knew that poison needed to go down the drain, but there was a darker force in his head battling to send it down his throat. Kevin's reflection in the glass bottle stared back at him as he contemplated his next move, then the hairs on the back of his neck stood straight up.

A sinister, raspy voice inside his head bellowed a drawn out, *Doooo it...* Kevin's heart stopped beating, as his gaze slowly rose from the reflection in hand, to the reflection in the mirror. The Kevin that was looking back at himself was no longer the same, but a twisted, malevolent being had taken his place. His eyes were like onyx marbles and his teeth were bared with an emotionless look on his face. Trembling with fear, Kevin saw the beast's lips begin to move in the mirror, as the voice in his head continued in a sickening tone, *Drink it all down, let it set you free.* He stood like stone and stared deep into its eyes. He knew that, in a way, this was the creature that killed Jacob, and now it wanted to complete the job. *Finish what you started, and your torment will end. Now drink.* The words were cryptic, but Kevin understood them completely; upon raising the glass bottle in hand, so did a putrid grin raise on the demon's face.

Kevin was ready for death but with that came a courage he hadn't experienced before, unlike anything alcohol had been able to conjure up. All he had to do was finish the bottle and finish what he started, but he refused to let this evil win. Kevin was going to finish what he started alright, but it would be on his terms. He smiled at the distorted figure and whispered, "Cheers," as the bottle tipped into the sink, and the rum began swirling down the drain.

The beast let out a deafening howl that shook the walls around him like an earthquake. The light fixture above his head swung violently, flickering on

and off as the drywall began to crack and crumble down from the ceiling. A black steam emitted from the skin of the creature and poured out from behind the edges of the mirror. Kevin turned to run, but time stood still. In his last waking moment, an explosion of glass shards flew past his head in slow motion, embedding themselves like knives into the door frame he was still trying to escape through. Small searing pains were tearing through his back and arms as time continued to slow.

Inching his way forward, the sound of the howl dulled to a low hum and faint voices echoed around him. Scenes from his past were playing out in the reflections of the broken glass. Christmas as a child, New Year's fireworks, his father's funeral, his wedding day – along with hundreds of others – were all projecting their own corresponding emotion. One stood out above all the others but was the least familiar. It was the image of a young girl in pajamas, holding a teddy bear, but Kevin couldn't remember where he had seen her before. His attention was shifted to a large piece of glass that silently sailed across the top of his right shoulder, slicing its way past his ear. This shard carried the image of the Deer that had been guiding him through this never-ending psychosis, but he was running away, escaping the blaze of a burning field.

Now Kevin was completely frozen in time,

and the nightmarish vapors bled past and consumed every memory from within each fragment of glass. The smoke slowly crept around him, a dense fog hugging the floor and building upon itself. It filled the room like a flood of black, soapy suds. It was cold and heavy, stealing the air from his lungs and leaving no room for the slightest breath. As the fog rose to completely consume Kevin, all feeling, sound, and emotion were lost. Only the smoke remained as it poured over the top of his head and sealed the look of terror on his face. Into the darkness once more.

Kevin's eyes were open the whole time in a trance-like state. It seemed to have been only a few moments before consciousness caught up with his stare, but long enough for him to sober up. He was standing in a grassy field, just before dawn. The mist was thick, and visibility went only a few yards ahead, but resting at the farthest reach of his sight was the silhouette of the Deer. Maybe it was an illusion, but there he was, waiting. Kevin carefully stepped forward to get closer, and a feeling in his gut told him he wasn't going anywhere this time. The Deer's rack of antlers looked as though it had doubled since Kevin last saw him. Motionless and calm, the chill of the morning air gave way to the steam rising from his velvety coat and the hot breath that pulsed from each side of his snout.

There was a brief moment of silence before Kevin addressed the Deer with a plea for help. "I am lost," he said in despair. "I don't know whether I'm alive or dead, whether I'm sick or well. I can barely remember where I've been, and it feels like years since I've slept. Please… show me the way back home." Silence persisted as the Deer held his sculpture-like stance and gazed back at him, seemingly unfazed by the address. "Hello? Can you hear me? I said I need help! I can't do this anymore."

The Deer never flinched but began to speak from within as he did before. The voice said, *You are alive and well but that is a matter of perception. The help you seek must come from within, along with the truth that leads to the end of your path.*

"What truth?" he asked, "Why is this happening to me? It's beginning to feel like one big, pointless dream."

The Deer bent down to nibble on a tuft of grass before continuing, *Soon you will be confronted with the evil that is so closely intertwined with your spirit. You must face yourself or drift as you have drifted forever more.*

Kevin fell silent. His expression dampened because, for once, he knew what the Deer meant. Whatever had been following him – that shadow at the edge of the swamp, the monstrous patient in the asylum, even his own reflection – was the evil he was referring to. Trying to make sense of it all was pointless. Kevin had been through too much to try and tie reason to it, although he thought, probably like most people do, that he was a fairly decent human being. How could there be evil in his spirit? He never hurt people or stole anything in his life, and he tried to go out of the way to help others whenever possible.

"How do I face myself?" he asked. "I definitely don't want to drift forever, so please point me in the right direction. Am I supposed to confront that creature? Is that creature me? What am I supposed to do?"

The Deer turned toward the fog to walk away before answering, *The path is already under your feet. All that is required is to keep moving forward. Remember to look within.*

With his final statement, the majestic animal walked away and disappeared into the dense mist. Kevin didn't bother following this time, the Deer was making a habit of delivering a cryptic message, then vanishing into thin air. He looked at the palms of his hands and thought of his past, wondering what he could have done to have such a disgusting presence following him around.

It was becoming clear that Kevin needed to take a fearless moral inventory of himself in order to move forward. Maybe he had missed something or forgotten part of his past. He had already forgotten so much that just thinking of what it could be was terrifying. His attention was broken by a mild vibration coming from around his feet, which intensified into a rumbling tremor.

Small fissures parted the grass into patches as the soil softened, and Kevin began to sink. Like quicksand, he plunged into the ground, waist deep, grasping at clumps of grass to keep from slipping farther. The earth opened its jaws and in an instant he was sucked into a tangled net of roots and vines, pulling him deeper and deeper into the ground. Kevin gasped and coughed as the sediment filled his lungs and eyes. In the midst of being buried alive, a brief wave of deja vu came – he had been here before.

Darkness and silence put an end to his struggling, and the weight of the once crushing soil became like that of a translucent fluid. As Kevin drifted downward into the abyss, the tips of his fingers crumbled and meshed with the hollow dirt around him. Limb by limb, bone by bone, his body broke apart and deposited into the earth above as he continued to sink. A femur and a few ribs drifted upward as the earth completely washed him away, like a sand castle clinging to the edge of a beach, until high tide swallows it for good.

Chapter 7
Roxanna

Pencil pushing, stiff collar,
Bar what's good to make a dollar.

The lecture hall was a dimly lit and depressing scene. What natural light managed to shine through the windows was limited by the dismal weather outside. The smell of burnt coffee and pine cleaner radiated from the back of the room. Roxanna stood at attention just after presenting the promising findings of her research to the board. She waited patiently as the board director shuffled papers and whispered back and forth with board members before delivering their response.

"Miss Dahlia, you've proven your point. As the Chief of Research on this project, I think we can all agree that you've worked the hardest of anyone else at the KAN Research Facility. Although you've provided plenty of research backing up your theories, you've still been unsuccessful. It would be folly for us to approve further funding for the project if we still can't make a connection with the patient in the subconscious. Now we've determined the positive effects on their behavior in the waking world, but unless something changes overnight, we are going to have to discontinue funding. I'm terribly sorry, we know this must be a devastating blow, but this field of science is simply too underdeveloped to make any further investments.

"Please don't take this personally, Miss Dahlia. Your hard work and determination to help the cognitively deficient hasn't gone unnoticed, and we are not saying that funding can't be reinstated in the future, given a significant breakthrough is made, but we don't see that happening anytime soon. Thank you for understanding."

Roxanna stood in disbelief, trying to comprehend the unexpected conclusion of the presentation she spent the last year preparing. Roxanna stared at the board members for a brief moment before responding.

"So that's it? You're telling me that I've toiled the last four years of my life only to be cut off at the knees? There are millions of people who could

benefit from this research, people who suffer daily from mental and emotional traumas and disorders, and you're telling me they will continue to suffer because of a potential financial risk? You're acting like I'm not aware of just how deep the pockets of KAN are, and I'll be damned if I'll believe this isn't important enough of a cause for you.

"Dr. Kellen, are you just going to sit there and say nothing? You were the one who said this would be a surefire win for further research, but now you're tucking your tail at the first sign of resistance?" Her mentor Dr. Kellen stayed silent and continued to stare at his shoes. He dared not look up and catch Roxanna's icy gaze.

The board director interjected before Roxanna could continue, "Now, now, Miss Dahlia, there's no need to use profanity. We are all professionals here. If you must know, Dr. Kellen has elected to donate funding from his own pocket to keep the project alive, although this means he will be the new Chief of Research going forward. The board agrees that his efforts leading in the direction of pharmaceutical development are in the best interest of KAN anyway."

"Are you kidding me?! My gut was right about you all along, Kellen! You acted like a friend long enough for me to trust you, only to use me for the heavy lifting in the lab. And now you are going to steal my work and claim all the credit and glory for yourself, aren't you? I knew you were only in this for the money, you snake! This is far from over!" Roxanna snarled.

The board watched in silence as she hastily packed her notebooks away and shuffled toward the exit in the back of the room, raising a middle finger high above her head as she slammed the door to the lecture hall on her way out.

Roxanna stormed down the hallway and began to rant. Her assistant Jamie had been waiting outside listening in on the ordeal. "Ughh! I'm sick of this, Jamie! Everything is one step forward and two steps back with these people. This research is solid, and they know it! This could be the breakthrough humanity has been looking for in neuroscience all along, and of course Kellen is stabbing me in the back! Things like dementia and schizophrenia would be a thing of the past, and they want to pull the plug because of a funding shortage?! Ughhh!"

"I know, Roxy. I had high hopes this time… all those countless hours and sleepless nights for nothing. If only we could give them hard proof that the research is finally paying off, like having one of them experience it for themselves, but none of them would ever take the time to practice lucidity and the techniques needed to make the jump," Jamie said.

"Well, we are not finished by a long shot, we've been teetering on the edge of a major breakthrough, and it's going to happen tonight, mark my words, Jamie. I'm not going to let Kellen win," Roxanna responded.

"Uhhhh… what does that mean, Roxy? This sounds illegal," Jamie asked.

"It might be, but I don't care. I'm not closing the door on this project without one more jump. Mrs. Klyde in psych ward B agreed to another session last week, she doesn't need to know about our presentation today. I've got one last theory to test out. If all goes well, then we will be back on track with the project and the board will have no choice but to reinstate our funding." The two of them came to the end of the hall they had been marching down and Roxanna stopped just before the door leading to the parking lot. She said to Jamie, "Meet me in the lab around nine, I'll bring Mrs. Klyde and get everything set up. You grab your tape recorder, some food, and a pack of party balloons."

"Party balloons?" Jamie asked with an inquisitive look on her face.

"Yes, pick up a pizza or something and prepare to stay in the lab for a while… it's going to be a long night." Roxanna answered.

With that the two went their separate ways and headed to their cars in the parking lot. Roxanna walked up to her 1963 VW Beetle and grabbed the keys from her purse, but she paused when she saw her reflection in the driver's side window. It was sinking in. This was it. All of her hard work over the last four years might have been for nothing. It stirred up an empty feeling in her stomach. She took a breath, opened the door, and drove home.

A few hours later, Jamie was walking up the steps to the lab, when she heard loud shouts: "Who are you?! How did I get here?!" Jamie hustled the rest of the way to the lab to find out what was going on. She scrambled with the pizza and bags she had to get the door open, only to find Mrs. Klyde backed up to one wall with a lamp in her hands, ready to swing if anyone got too close. Roxanna was on the other side of the room trying to calm her down.

"Mrs. Klyde, please calm down! Just breathe! No one is going to hurt you!" Roxanna exclaimed to no avail.

Jamie came into the room, dropped everything on the counter, and asked, "Roxanna, what did you do?! Why is she freaking out?"

Roxanna replied, "I stopped by her room and explained the situation to her and that we needed her help one last time. She was more than happy to help."

"Then why is she losing it right now?!" Jamie asked.

Before Roxanna answered, Mrs. Klyde became silent. She lowered the lamp and asked, "Is that pizza?"

Jamie said, "Why yes, it is, Mrs. Klyde! You can have as much as you want, but you must calm down, promise?" She looked back and forth at the two women, slowly set the lamp on the floor, and cautiously walked over to the counter with the pizza box. Roxanna and Jamie looked at each other in silence. Jamie walked over to Roxanna as Mrs. Klyde began devouring the pizza, slice by slice. Jamie whispered to her, "Is she not on her meds?"

"Well… I may have convinced her not to take her evening dose… I want to know if the medication has an impact on lucidity possibilities," said Roxanna.

"Are you kidding me, Roxy? Don't you realize how unethical that is? Let alone illegal on so many levels!" Jamie exclaimed.

"Shhhh! Keep your voice down, Jamie, she's finally calm. I think the pizza was a good call though. At this point, all we need to have is one more trial run… think of it as routine. We are in the thick of it now, I'm not going to accept defeat until we've gone down every possible avenue. You need to tell me right now, are you in? Or are you out?" Roxanna replied.

Jamie looked over at the woman scarfing down their dinner, leaned up against the wall, and stared at her feet. After a brief moment of silence, she sighed and said, "I'm in it till the end, Roxy."

A smile of reassurance came over Roxanna's face before she turned to Mrs. Klyde to say, "Okay, Mrs. K, whenever you're ready we can get started with the testing. You know the drill, just lie down on the monitoring bench and Jamie will get you hooked up to the equipment." Mrs. Klyde finished her fourth slice of pizza and walked over to the testing area, where Jamie was already pulling out electrodes from the drawer. Mrs. Klyde laid down on the bench and got as comfortable as she could while Jamie began attaching the electrodes.

Roxanna walked over to her preparation area where she would take a melatonin supplement to help her fall asleep faster and put some headphones on to listen to calming music. Through her research, she discovered that meditation helped her drop into a lucid dream much faster and so it became common practice before every trial for the last four years. Just a few deep breaths and her mind began emptying all the thoughts and stressors that were floating around. The bad news about her project, the uncertainty of the future, and most of all, the repercussions of her actions. Roxanna had learned that an empty mind was imperative to becoming lucid.

Jamie had time to finally enjoy a piece of pizza for dinner. She looked over at Roxanna sitting cross-legged in her comfy chair while she took a bite and thought to herself, *What have I gotten myself into? I hope Roxy knows what she's doing, because our careers and potentially our freedom are on the line.*

About twenty minutes went by and Mrs. Klyde was already snoring her way through a cheese coma when Roxanna finally opened her eyes and removed her headphones. "Are we ready?" she asked Jamie in a whisper from across the room.

"Now or never," Jamie answered. Roxanna quietly stood up and made her way over to the second monitoring bench next to her patient. Roxanna's eyes were getting heavy, and Jamie attached the last electrode as she drifted off to sleep.

Roxanna opened her eyes and sat up in a cold sweat. She was groggy, but she could tell that she had awakened on top of a flat boulder overhanging a babbling brook in the mountains with pine trees all around, and the air was crisp like an early spring morning. Birds were chirping here and there in synchronicity with an orchestra of crickets and other insects off in the distance. Roxanna collected herself and went straight to looking for Mrs. Klyde. As long as she kept Mrs. Klyde's image in her mind, eventually Roxanna could manifest her location. The problem so far in her research and trials was that she couldn't bridge the connection with her patients in both the subconscious and the conscious. Proving she could make that connection with someone after they woke up was always what held up progress.

Roxanna had gotten so good at lucid dreaming that she could transport herself to any location, manifest any object, and defy the laws of gravity all by only using her mind. Despite these profound abilities she had within her own dreams, she was very limited in what she could control in someone else's dream. The cold, hard proof that she was looking for to defend her dissertation was elusive at every turn. All that was required was to be able to communicate with the test subject and have them remember exactly what was said to them, and if she could accomplish this, it was only a matter of a controlled, monitored experiment with her professor and a board member present to testify to the success. That wouldn't be possible if she couldn't even get the test subject to remember. If she could prove the connection was possible, then Roxanna was confident that KAN would continue to fund her research and approve her therapy methods on future patients. It could lead to a major breakthrough in cognitive regeneration, but every possible influence on memory had already been exhausted – sound, smell, touch, temperature – except for color. It was the only idea she had left to try.

Roxanna collected her thoughts and closed

her eyes to focus on every detail she remembered about Mrs. Klyde. Her hair, her clothes, the pizza she was munching on, everything she could conjure within her mind would help with the jump from her dream to Mrs. Klyde's. She took a few deep breaths and slowly opened her eyes to find herself standing in the middle of a cobblestone courtyard surrounded by ancient buildings, perhaps Italian architecture. Mrs. Klyde was at the other end of the courtyard examining the walls and stonework in a typical tourist outfit with a camera.

"Fancy meeting you here, Miss Dahlia, what took you so long?" she said without looking.

Roxanna paused and examined Mrs. Klyde before responding. Something was already very different about this encounter compared to the previous tests she had performed with her. Normally Roxanna would find her in nature, like a forest or a poppy field, but this time it felt much more personal. She also didn't communicate very much, now Mrs. Klyde was the one starting the conversation.

"Sorry to keep you waiting! Sometimes it can be challenging getting from one spot to the next in our dreams. I'm glad to see you in such high spirits, Mrs. K! We haven't spoken in a place like this until now, is it important to you in some way? Maybe a memory?" Roxanna asked.

Mrs. Klyde turned her head to make eye

contact and her face slowly sank into distant despair. "My husband and I came to Venice for our tenth anniversary. Even after all that time we were still madly in love, and we made a tradition of coming to Italy every couple of years to relive our adventures together. We must have made the journey seven or eight more times to see these old structures and enjoy the food, but also just to enjoy each other's company. I lost him five years back to a heart attack. I just… well, I never expected to lose him. One day we were planting new hydrangeas in the front flower beds, and the next day he was gone… We promised each other that we would be together forever, but life has a sick sense of humor sometimes… it dangles a carrot in front of your face, then it lets you nibble just long enough to make you unable to live without it. Then it snatches it away when you least expect it." Mrs. Klyde's demeanor changed as she answered.

"I'm… I'm so sorry to hear that, Mrs. K. I don't really know what it's like to lose a loved one, especially a husband, so I won't pretend that I understand. It sounds like you two really loved each other. Now, Mrs. K, we might not have a lot of time together in this capacity, so I'd like to get started working on developing your dream recall. I've brought some balloons with me and all I need you to do is examine every detail of them. You are going to be imprinting them deep in your memory, and hopefully you can pull the memory from your subconscious when you wake up. Tell me, what's your favorite color?" Roxanna asked.

Mrs. Klyde, now staring at the ground beneath her feet, looked up and replied, "Green, my favorite color is green… why?" Roxanna pulled a small baggie out of her back pocket and shuffled through it until she found a green balloon.

She started blowing up the balloon as Mrs. Klyde's demeanor continued to deteriorate. Roxanna watched her as her expression went from confused to annoyed, and as she tied off the balloon, Roxanna responded, "Okay, I'm not sure if this is going to work, but this is my only remaining theory to test. All I need you to do is focus on this balloon for the rest of your dream – now I know that sounds boring, but it has to keep your attention the entire time. You need to examine everything about it and nothing else."

Mrs. Klyde took the balloon from her and stared at it with the same disgruntled look on her face, but she kept looking back at the cobblestone wall in front of her. Roxanna noticed dark clouds were forming above the courtyard and the rumble of thunder was approaching from the north. Roxanna was about to try and wake herself up to give Mrs. Klyde time to herself, but something was wrong. Roxanna watched silently as Mrs. Klyde looked back and forth from the wall to the green balloon until she lowered her hand and let it fall to the ground. Her fists clenched as the clouds darkened and swirled overhead. Rain drops began to peck at the ground as Mrs. Klyde started breathing heavily and tears started flowing from the corners of her eyes. The thunder was upon them as Roxanna looked on in confusion. She had never experienced such a phenomenon. It seemed as though the weather was being directly influenced by the dreamer's emotions, and those emotions were crumbling by the second. Mrs. Klyde was grinding her teeth together as the wind picked up and the rain started coming down in sheets.

They were both getting soaked when the ground started to shake. Roxanna tried to console her but to no avail. Mrs. Klyde started wailing and screaming at the wall, elevating the weather to a full-fledged hurricane. Roxanna lost her footing in the quake and fell to the ground as bricks and stones started tumbling down toward them from the top of the wall. Mrs.Klyde screamed louder and louder, breaking the earth apart around them. Roxanna was terrified, having no idea what to do; she heard a voice echoing past the roaring thunder, "Roxy… ROXY! Please… WAKE UP!" Mrs. Klyde fell to her knees, crying in agony as the wind blew the balloon back around the courtyard, just past Roxanna's head before popping with a deafening blow, then silence.

Roxanna sat up in a whirlwind, heart racing and sweating profusely. She pulled all the electrodes from her skin and got off the monitoring bench when Jamie said, "My gosh, Roxy! Are you okay? What happened in there?!"

"I'm not sure yet, but it was a failure for sure, Jamie. Everything was going fine, but her dream was influenced by the memory of her late husband. She just lost it and a hurricane started destroying everything! It was definitely due to the emotional toll it took on her, but now I have so many more questions than I started with. We may not have any idea what we are dealing with here," Roxanna shook her head and turned her attention to her patient.

Mrs. Klyde was still squirming on the bench in that nightmare – Roxy and Jamie went to either side of her to wake her up and calm her down. Suddenly, Mrs. Klyde's eyes opened, letting go of a stream of tears. Roxanna leaned in and grabbed her hand to console her. She said, "Mrs. K, I'm so sorry, that must have been much worse for you than it was for me. Now I have to ask, can you—"

Mrs. Klyde cut her off before she could finish her sentence and said, "Green… the balloon was green. Can I go home now?"

Roxy and Jamie looked up at each other with an equal look of awe. Jamie asked, "Does that mean it worked?!"

Chapter 8
Rock Bottom

Arid land, it's not too late,
Confront your past, seal your fate.

A tiny pebble fell from the ceiling of a damp cavern. It bounced off Kevin's forehead and jolted him awake. He was lying in a soft pile of silt and sediment, but there was no opening above his head. A blue glow emitted from the perimeter of the cavern, seemingly coming from small crystal-like structures that protruded from the floor and walls. Kevin sat up and noticed a red glow coming from the end of a tunnel. Rising to his feet brought on a storm of coughing that sent him back to his knees. Finally expelling the dust and grime from his lungs, Kevin composed himself and headed toward the red glow.

The tunnel was narrow, and if it wasn't for the fluorescent crystalline formations, he'd have been tripping over his own feet. He was weary, but the words of the Deer kept his mission in perspective. It's all he had to hold on to, and the only consistency so far. Everything Kevin had been through felt like distant memories or dreams. The farther his journey took him, the less he could remember, and he could no longer differentiate fact from fantasy. The beginning felt like decades ago; where Kevin began, where he came from, even his last name was lost. It was all an enigma.

The air in the crystalline cave was cool and damp, although the temperature was rising with each step, and a dryness was forming in the back of his throat. He was getting closer to the red glow and could see now that it was coming from an exit to this cave system, leading outside. A hot breeze was blowing into the mouth of the cave like an oven. Kevin stepped to the opening and placed his hand on the wall of the cave for support. The scene was menacing, like that of a clay canyon turned hellscape. He looked down on an arid wasteland that stretched as far as the eye could see. The red glow was the sky behind smoky clouds, reflecting what he could only assume was a large fire off in the distance. A hill of sandstone and slate rock piled up to the edge of the cave and led down into a valley with clay, cliff-like walls on either side. Kevin worked his way down to the valley floor; pebbles and bits of slate followed with each step descending the rocky mound. Simply put, it was a land of true desolation.

Between the valley walls, a narrow passageway led deeper into the canyon. Dead roots and shriveled vines crawled out of cracks and crevices in the rock on either side. He paused for a moment, and to his surprise and equal alarm, he could hear the sound of two people talking in the distance. *Why do I know those voices?* he thought to himself, making his way through the sandstone corridor. The path was winding; some stretches headed uphill only to dip back down through areas that might have once carried water – ridges and sediment deposits were all that remained now. The voices got louder with each step forward. Kevin still couldn't make out what they were saying, but one was male and the other female.

Around the last bend in the valley, he had seemingly come to a dead end. He might have turned back if it wasn't for a handful of glowing, red rays of light shining past a large cluster of dead vines hanging over an opening in the rock. He began tugging at the dried up, rope-like roots, and the voices that seemed to be coming from the other side halted. "Shhhh! What was that?" the man said.

Kevin continued pulling down the obstruction when the woman said, "It's coming from over there..." He cleared the way and squeezed through an opening that led to a wide-open patch of ground on the edge of a cliff. The hike through the arid environment had him winded, the dust and hot air made his lungs feel like canister vacuum bags that had been sucking up drywall dust all day.

Taking a brief moment to catch his breath, Kevin's attention was jolted to the right by the sound of a safety switching to fire on a high-powered hunting rifle. There stood a middle-aged man, pointing the business end of a .308 right at him. Next to the man was a younger woman with black hair in medical scrubs. She had tattoos running up and down her arms, and the look on her face was much more receptive.

"Kevin?! Is that you?" the man said as he lowered his gun.

It was Roxanna and Jacob. Kevin was overwhelmed with relief and joy, and he fell to his knees. "Thank you, God..." he whispered. His memory had been fading every time he opened his eyes in a new world, but he remembered them, only bits and pieces, but enough to know they were here to help.

"I told you we would find him here," Roxanna said to Jacob as she walked over, extending a hand to help Kevin to his feet.

"Where... what... how did you guys get here? Jacob, I thought you were a goner, man." he asked as Jacob lowered a familiar leather bag from his shoulder, along with the horn, blade, and water pouch.

"I was, but I just woke up the next morning like nothing had ever happened, only I could remember everything. Nurse Dahlia helped me get out, and we've been looking for you ever since. Here, you can carry this now. I've been hauling it around for days," Jacob replied. Kevin snatched up the chilled canteen and guzzled pint after pint until his thirst was quenched. A quick splash over the top of his head was refreshing as it trickled past his ears and soaked his shoulders. He turned to Jacob with a confused look on his face.

"Days... what do you mean days? How long has it been since that looney bin?" Kevin asked.

Roxanna chimed in, "It hasn't been a week yet, but I suspect it's been much longer for you. Time works very differently in the subconscious. What feels like months here only lasts about a day in reality."

"It's been years for me..." Kevin said under his breath; but if that was true, then it hadn't been nearly as long as he thought. There was a chance that his downward spiral in that dismal apartment was another manifestation of his own mind, and Katie could still be out there somewhere waiting for him. It was a hopeful thought, enough for Kevin to grit his teeth once more and carry on. The longer he spoke to the two of them, the more fragments of memories came flooding back – like the medical tests and the pit he fell into on the first day of work. "I have to face that evil from the asylum… I think it's the only way I can get back home. He's here somewhere," Kevin said while equipping his gear and tightening the shoulder straps of the backpack.

Jacob said, "Nurse Dahlia says we all got somethin' holding us back, something we have to finish before we can escape this hell, like a mission."

Kevin looked at Roxanna as she spoke, "It's true. Although I haven't had much success with my test subjects in the way of lucid dreaming, I've been working closely with a colleague whose patients suffer from a wide range of psychological conditions. He treats his patients with a form of hypnotherapy that forces the individual to examine themselves and the very core of their being – life experiences, memories, trauma, all the good and bad that make us who we are. He claims that the majority of the patients who made a full recovery, or at least those who returned to a relatively sane state of mind, pointed out that they had to come face to face with elements of their lives that had been buried for a long time. Suppressed memories if you will. If that darkness from the asylum is yours, then we will help you face it."

Her words reassured Kevin of his quest. "Thank you, friends… Something tells me I'm going to need the help," he said, giving Jacob a humbled look. "I'm sorry I left you behind…"

Jacob looked back and smiled, "Don't worry about it, kid, I woulda done the same thing, haha! Besides, it didn't make sense for both of us to get thrashed by that goober. I'm here all the same, now let's get after him."

Kevin looked around and noticed another narrow path between the edge of the cliff and a wall of stone. What clearly was the only way forward was also an unnaturally long way down. He peered over the edge and gasped. After what looked like a mile or two of sheer ninety degree cliff face, the rest of the canyon simply vanished in a dense fog. There was no bottom in sight due to a reddish-gray haze hanging over the entire panorama, like a completely new atmosphere; it felt alien in a way. "Unfortunately, I think this is the way," Kevin said as the others followed behind. The way was treacherous, and each step had to be taken with calculated care. Sediment and pebbles slid off the edge of the path, creating an ominous "this could be you" kind of feeling. The path, which was only a few feet wide, was fairly straight at least and led to another cliff-side plateau. The three of them were silent as the grave as they crossed the sculpted catwalk, until Kevin piped up to say, "Almost there." In an instant, he was startled by Jacob letting out a shriek of terror as a portion of sandstone crumbled underneath his feet.

Jacob's chest slammed into the edge of the path as he scrambled for something to grasp on to. "Jacob!" Roxanna cried out as she dove to the edge to catch a hand, but he was already gone. Their hearts were in their stomachs as Kevin and Roxanna peered over the edge as quickly as possible. There, by the chance of a chance, was Jacob holding on to the shoulder strap of his rifle, which had wedged itself in a crevice that opened up four or five feet down. He looked up at them with a silent look of terror and dangled like a marionette with only one string left.

"Hold on!" Kevin shouted as Roxanna reached her arm down, but he was too far away.

"I can't reach him!" shouted Roxanna as the rifle dug into the soft clay and stone, slipping another few inches.

"Hurry! I'm slipping!" Jacob cried, as Kevin struggled to find a solution. Finally, seconds that felt like minutes led to the epiphany of the net he had stowed in his bag for emergencies like this one.

With one fluid motion, Kevin reached over his shoulder into the leather bag and grabbed a handful of the silvery mesh. Tossing it over the edge of the cliff, it draped around Jacob's shoulders. "Grab hold, Jacob!" he shouted as he unsheathed the hunting knife and drove it deep into the ground to grip for leverage. Roxanna tangled the other side of the net in her arms and leaned back to help support the weight. Violent tugging and thrashing ensued as Jacob took hold of the net and began his climb.

"Hold on! We've got you!" Roxanna shouted again as one hand came over the ledge, tossing the rifle to one side. Another hand, then a forearm, elbow, and shoulder, until Jacob was able to shimmy his way up and back onto the path, where they all collapsed wearily.

After a minute of heavy breathing, Jacob chuckled, "Let's not do that again," – a welcome comic relief made them laugh as they proceeded on all fours to get to the other side. They weren't taking any chances after that.

One by one they poured out of the pathway in celebration, hugging and cheering, grateful that their comrade hadn't fallen into the abyss. "Man! Was that net in the bag the whole time?! Where'd you get that thing!" Jacob exclaimed.

Kevin laughed and replied, "You wouldn't believe me if I told you, but it's probably the only time walking into a spider web has paid off for me."

Roxanna looked past them with a bewildered

look on her face and asked in a quieted voice, "Wait... who is that?" Kevin turned to see what looked like a corpse leaning against a dead tree that probably dried up a long time ago. It was a frail woman, maybe thirty-five, she was still alive, but barely.

"Ma'am, are you okay?" Jacob asked as the three of them approached. Head hung low, and arms laying in the dirt, she gave no response.

"Where did you come from?" Kevin asked as he extended his leather canteen in her direction. Her feeble hands reached out and grabbed it. She tipped it upward, spilling the ice-cold water everywhere with each miniscule sip she managed to take. She barely had the strength to hold it steady as her skeletal arms began to tremble. Her silence was maintained as they questioned further. Another memory came through, and Kevin reached into the bag to reveal a handful of half-smushed blueberries. "Here, eat this," he said as she slowly set the water down and reached out again with cupped palms. He poured the berries into her hands, and Roxanna finally asked a question that got somewhat of a response.

"Can you tell us your name?" she asked, as the woman slowly started chewing on the blueberries one by one.

Through the attempt of eating, a weak voice produced an answer, "I'm... my name. I'm not sure..."

"That's okay, sweetie, can you stand? We are going to get out of this place – you should come with us," Roxanna replied.

"Uhhh… are you sure that's a good idea? We don't know anything about this girl, why is she even here?" Jacob interjected.

"Jacob, she's here, isn't she? Which means this woman is trapped just like you. You three are in the same boat. There's a chance she can escape too, but only if we help her," Roxanna answered.

"I ain't too sure 'bout this, what d'ya think, Kevin?" Jacob asked.

"I'm not sure about it either, but we definitely can't leave her here. Who knows how long she's been baking like this." And with that, the frail woman slowly rose to her feet and outstretched one arm to point a finger at another pathway through the rocks.

"The way out… it's this way…" she said and began shuffling in that direction. Jacob, Roxanna, and Kevin all looked at each other in bewilderment, but they all silently agreed she could help.

Heading down the path in single file, they could only travel at the stranger's pace. It wasn't long before Jacob piped up, "Hey, wait, if you know the way out, why ain't you just left already?" The stranger stopped dead in her tracks, causing the three of them to bump into one another.

She slowly turned her head and tears were

forming in her eyes, "The darkness won't let me leave... and it won't let me die..." She then turned and continued leading them down the path. The unnerving message caused a bit of hesitation in the group, but only for a moment.

Jacob, who was in the back, said, "I've got a real bad feeling about this. I hope "darkness" don't mean what I think it means..."

"I feel the same way," Kevin whispered under his breath.

Down through the chasm they hiked until they found another opening leading out of the canyon and farther into the barren wastes beyond. The ground was flat and stretched thirty or forty yards before a layer of tall, dead grass continued in the expanse. The only noticeable features were dried up cracks that spread across the dusty ground, as if this land was once home to a large body of water that had long since evaporated. "Well, it looks like we made it out of that godforsaken canyon, but tell me we ain't gotta keep trudging across this desert..." Jacob asked the woman. She didn't answer.

The woman began to shake and fell to her knees sobbing. "Please forgive me... please, God, forgive me," the woman whispered as she wept.

Roxanna ran to her side to console her and asked, "What's wrong? Forgive you for what?"

The frail stranger slowly looked up into

Roxanna's eyes and whispered from her cracked lips, "The darkness made me do it…"

A trembling began to rise up from the earth beneath their feet. Pebbles danced across the clay and fell into the spiderweb of cracks all around as the tremble became a quake with a deafening sound. "What's going on?!" Jacob shouted only a few yards away, but Kevin could barely even hear him. Black smoke poured from the openings in the earth everywhere. It rose up like walls of tar, separating the group and trapping them in their own patches of clay.

"Don't touch it!" Kevin shouted before losing sight of Jacob and Roxanna completely. The smoke rose higher and rolled over itself, sealing him into the darkness. All the rumbling instantly stopped and there was silence. The once dry heat of the environment had become frigid cold. "Can you hear me?! Hello?!" Kevin yelled again, but no response, only silence.

The black walls began to shimmer, like the surface of water, and a scene of a suburban roadway with houses and mailboxes on either side was forming before his eyes . It was nighttime, and the road seemed familiar to him. A little girl, maybe nine years old, walked out into the road and looked directly at Kevin with anger in her eyes. The sight struck a nerve deep down in his heart. He tried to look away, but the darkness compelled him to watch. A bright light shone on her, showing the set of matching unicorn pajamas she was wearing and the teddy bear she was holding in her right hand. A half second later, she let out a shriek of terror as she was wiped from the street by a speeding white truck that Kevin recognised all too well.

A flood of memory and remorse came crashing in as he fell to his knees. His heart sank, because now the reality was setting in that he may have done something horrible. The smoke began to recede and trickle back down into the earth, and the red glowing light of the sky shined down on Kevin once more. He looked around and saw Jacob curled up on the ground, whimpering and mumbling. Roxanna seemed to be unscathed, but where the stranger once laid was a gaping pit in the ground, as if the darkness had swallowed her whole.

"Kevin! Are you okay?" Roxanna asked as he managed to stand.

"I think so... help Jacob," he responded. Another smaller trembling ensued as the black smoke emerged from the ground once more, forming a silhouette of the evil being that had been stalking him. Its blood red eyes opened and locked on to Kevin immediately.

"We need to move! Back to the canyon!" Roxanna shouted as she raised Jacob to his feet and helped him back to the opening in the rock. Before they could enter, the smoky resin shot out of the walls of the path, blocking the way in. She looked back at Kevin with a look that implied all hope was lost.

He lowered his shoulder bag to the ground and retrieved the drinking flask to take one last sip of the ice-cold spring water and then dropped it to the ground. He undid the buckle of the belt with his father's horn. He gripped the bone handle of the hunting knife, unsheathing it as he let the belt fall to the ground. Off in the distance behind the demon, he saw a figure slowly approach and pause. It was the majestic Deer that had brought him this far, and there was another unknown force with him. They were too far off to tell, but their presence was calming, and it felt like a good omen.

Kevin was ready to fight, and he was ready to die. Running was no longer an option, and he couldn't help but feel this was the end of his journey. The sins of his past had been buried for too long, and it was time to atone. The beast glared at him with an evil grin from ear to ear. Kevin clenched his fists before taking one last deep breath and looked back at Roxanna to say, "I've got this…"

Despite the unavoidable terror of the situation at hand, he couldn't help but embrace this overwhelming sense of peace that was coming over him. It was the first time since the beginning of this journey that Kevin was content. Win or lose, he was done running, and this creature was about to get put in its place. The knife felt so natural in his hand, like this was the whole reason he had been carrying it around all this time. Kevin's heart began to race, and once more, adrenaline was imbuing him with the confidence he needed.

A swift lunge forward, and he attempted to send the blade into the belly of the beast, but its form was so fluid, that the shadow effortlessly dodged the attack. Kevin was knocked off balance and a right hook came flying into his ribcage, sending him face first into the dirt. He could hear the beast snickering as he gasped for air on the ground. He choked on the dust that made its way into his lungs, but he rose to his feet and swung the knife again, this time aiming for the throat. Yet again, the beast was too quick. This time an unseen fist came flying upwards into his chin. Kevin's jaw cracked as his head flew backwards. In the blink of an eye, he was lying on his back, staring up at the hazy sky while blood began pooling in his mouth. He had been in fights before, but each blow was taking so much out of him, as if they were sapping not only Kevin's energy, but his sheer will to live.

"Okay, Kevin..." he said under his breath as he gathered himself to his feet once more. The creature grinned and took one step forward. Kevin reacted and took his last chance to send the blade deep into its chest. Finally, he made contact, but the blade just passed through as if he was slicing through thin air. Kevin's knife disappeared, along with his hand and forearm, but he couldn't pull away. As if he had reached into hell itself, his arm was trapped and seared by what felt like not only fire but ice as well. The pain was so swift and intense, he couldn't even scream. Another well-timed strike to the gut sent Kevin backward, along with his now scorched forearm, and with that he was beaten. He fell to his knees, and began drawing his last breaths.

Everything was quiet as his eyesight slowly dimmed. Kevin's head hung low as the creature approached and began to speak. "You can't win... but you don't have to lose..." it hissed. Kevin looked up and saw an outstretched hand of gangly black fingers reaching out for him to take hold. What began as confidence was now true hopelessness. As if he was already possessed, his hand slowly raised and extended itself as if to accept defeat and allow the shadow to finally get what it wanted.

One last glimpse of the Deer changed everything. In that moment, every memory Kevin had lost came pouring in like a tsunami – the good along with the bad. The things he saw and the person he was in his past made one thing clear – he would rather die than embrace the evil that once flowed through his veins.

Without a second thought, he grasped the hunting knife, turned it on himself, and sent the blade into his own heart. The beast began writhing and scrambling in front of him as Kevin pulled air into his lungs for the last time and slumped over onto his side. As his eyes closed, his final thoughts were not of regret or shame, but of redemption and purpose fulfilled. He had killed the person he used to be, and in doing so, vanquished his demon.

Chapter 9
The Great Divide

*One wakes up, one falls asleep,
Which is which, in a dream this deep?*

Thomas opened his eyes, staring at the ceiling above. Lying still and quiet, he tried to recount every detail of the nightmare he had just experienced. It had been years since he had a dream this vivid. "Bizarre… I gotta lay off the cheese before bed," he said as he reached for the bottle of water on the nightstand. To his delight, the smell of coffee began filling the air. His wife was always up before the break of dawn to get her daily Zumba workout in, and he regretted never being up in time to spy on her. She was beautiful, and he knew just how lucky he was.

"Babe? You awake yet? I know it's Saturday and all, but you said you would come with me to the farmer's market," he heard her holler from the kitchen.

"Yes, dear..." he replied as he tumbled off the bed and zig-zagged down the hall, bouncing from one wall to the next for balance. Still half-asleep, the smell of coffee was guiding him even if his eyes weren't completely open yet.

"Here," Amy said as she handed him a cup of coffee.

"Thanks… man, oh man, did I have a strange dream last night," he responded.

"You have seemed restless the last couple of nights. What was it about?" she asked.

Thomas replied, "I don't totally remember, only bits and pieces, but I saw a treehouse in a strange forest. I also remember some sort of hospital, but I don't think they were the same dream."

"Weird, you should start writing them down, hun," Amy replied before adding, "As soon as you get dressed, we can head to the market and knock out a few errands before it gets too late in the day." With that, Thomas sipped on his coffee while getting ready, and they both got in the car and headed into town.

It was a beautiful Saturday morning on the country road that they took every day to and from work. Amy was a bank teller, and Thomas was one of the saw operators at the local mill. He loved the smell of fresh cut cedar but always wanted to start his own carpentry business putting a finer finish on the lumber he was so familiar with. Thomas had taken the last few weeks off work under doctor's orders, due to a head injury caused by a negligent coworker carrying a stack of milled boards that were clearly too heavy for him. One misstep and he stumbled forward, spearing Thomas in the side of the head. Apart from a minor concussion and a few stitches, the injury was healing nicely, and for once, workers' comp was doing its job.

A few minutes down the road, they were passing a large clearing of farmland on the right. Amy was driving, listening to her favorite supernatural podcast, when Thomas noticed something strange. There in the field, stood a large Deer watching them as they passed. "Whoa! Look at the size of that sucker!" he blurted out, startling Amy out of her cruising trance.

"What? Where?" she asked.

"That Deer in the field! What a rack!" he exclaimed.

"Why, thank you..." Amy replied with a quirky grin on her face. Thomas chuckled and assumed she just missed it. The more he thought about what he had just seen, an eerie feeling of confusion began to sink in. After a few more miles, they pulled into a large parking lot filled with vendor tents selling all kinds of produce and homemade goodies. His attention was quickly brought to the smell of the local barbecue pit that always showed up with a mobile smoker. They found a spot and folded themselves in with the rest of the crowd.

"I'm gonna go say hi to Tammy and pick up a few jars of that apple butter you love so much," Amy said to her entranced husband, currently drooling and floating toward the smoky aroma of pulled pork.

"That's nice, hun… I'm gonna get us some lunch…" he replied, as he walked up to the barbecue tent. Tammy didn't rank very high in his book. She had an intense personality, in your face and to the point. She was really the polar opposite of Thomas, and all too often made him very uncomfortable, although he did a good job of hiding it for Amy's sake. *"Innocent flirting,"* Amy called it, but Thomas had a feeling that there wasn't an ounce of innocence in that woman. He couldn't help admitting to himself that she was very attractive, and the bright red hair was the icing on the cake. All the more reason to avoid her at all costs.

"What do you want…" a burly, greasy man grumbled at him as Thomas snapped out of his thoughts and looked over the small menu hanging above the tent.

"I'll take two pork sandwiches please, but do you serve them with coleslaw?" Thomas said as the man gave him a sharp look.

"Does it say coleslaw anywhere on that menu?" the man replied.

"Huhhh... no?" said Thomas.

"Then the answer is no..." the man said in a sarcastic tone.

"Well damn, aren't you just a peach," Thomas replied as he traded cash for a greasy paper bag full of porky goodness. Despite the unpleasant interaction, as Thomas walked away, he couldn't help but feel like he had met the barbecue guy before; he couldn't put his finger on it. Was it in one of those dreams? Or maybe some type of deja vu? As he made his way back to Amy, stopping here and there to pick up a few ears of corn and beefsteak tomatoes, his sense of confusion flushed his brain when he noticed a tent selling nothing but the most plump and delicious looking blueberries he had ever seen.

All of a sudden, a searing pain shot up the back of his neck and pulsed across his skull. "Ughhh..." he moaned as his wife found him holding his head and trying to avoid sunlight.

"Babe, are you okay?" Amy asked as she grabbed hold of one arm, guiding him back to the car.

"It's just one of those headaches I've been

getting lately," he responded, slowly trying to climb into the passenger seat of the car.

"I think you need to see the doctor again," she said, "Wait here, and I'll finish up. The doctor said to swing by if they kept happening. I'm taking you in."

"Okay… okay… just let me close my eyes for a minute," he replied. Thomas knew there was no use in arguing with her when it came to his health; she cared about him. As she closed the car door, he realized the smell of the pork barbecue that he was just drooling over, was now nauseating him. Another shooting pain was all it took for him to force the car door open to vomit before slouching into the seat and drifting off into the darkness.

When Thomas came to, he found himself floating through the endless abyss that is the universe, but a sense of peace kept him from panic. He was warm, and the weightlessness he had never experienced before was euphoric. Arms stretched out in front of him, he drifted slowly toward a huge green planet, beautiful and perfect in its shape. He turned his head and noticed a few more planets behind him, some larger and some very far away. Before long, Thomas realized he was sailing on the outskirts of the solar system. When he turned back around, he was startled by the transformation of the green planet, which was no longer a planet at all, but a massive green stag head. Its antlers looked like the trunks of two giant oak trees with limbs that branched out by the hundreds, then thousands.

A booming voice began to speak in his mind, *You have been brought here for a reason not to be revealed by my wisdom, but by yours... A path has been placed beneath your feet that must be traveled. Every step taken will lead you to an understanding greater than yourself. Search within for the answers or be consumed by the questions...*

Thomas, still at ease, was also a bit unnerved by the experience, and responded, "This is a dream, it must be... You speak in lovely parables, but would you care to elaborate?" With a thunderous roar, the mouth of the celestial being began to open, and a bright light shined past its teeth. A force started to pull Thomas closer and closer, faster and faster. He couldn't help but scream as he flew like a bullet quicker than light itself, straight into the blinding maw.

The bright light subsided as Thomas opened his eyes. Nausea and a pounding headache woke him in a similar fashion as when they put him to sleep. A consequence all too reminiscent of his drinking days.

He found himself outstretched on the couch in the living room, and before he could think, his stomach curled him over the edge to lose its last meal on the carpet. "Ugh… what is that? Gross…" he uttered as he scanned the room. A familiar greasy paper bag was sitting on the end table. Barbecue usually led to the worst heartburn of his life due to a weak stomach lining, but he was a glutton for punishment. It was another consequence of overindulgence, but this was different. He couldn't even remember enjoying the bane of a meal.

"Hun! Are you okay?!" his wife called out, rushing into the room.

"What happened? All I remember is getting sick at the market." Tears began filling his eyes before asking one more question, "Please, God… Honey, tell me I didn't drink again…"

Amy left the room abruptly and returned with a towel to throw over the mess on the floor before sitting on the edge of the couch to embrace him. "No, baby, you didn't drink. But I do think you're very sick. That blow to the head may have done more damage than we thought. I took you to the doctor's office on the way home, but he wasn't in – of all times to be golfing! I insisted the nurse check your vitals, but you wouldn't wake up. She said it wasn't uncommon for a serious migraine to render someone unconscious, but you really scared me, babe… She sent me home with some medication and told me to bring you in on Monday for a brain scan." Thomas noticed the level of concern in her eyes and knew not to make a joke of the situation. She continued, "I didn't want to wake you up for church. You seemed to finally be resting well, and I figured we could watch online when you're feeling better."

"Church? Today is Sunday?! Are you saying I've been sleeping since yesterday morning?" he asked.

"Not exactly, you were in and out all evening, but definitely dazed. I managed to get you to eat and take a pill, but you fell asleep shortly after, so I let you rest." Thomas couldn't remember anything at all, but he was starting to feel better.

A few hours later, he managed to hold down a bowl of cereal and took another pill. As he lay on the couch watching cartoons, bits and pieces of the space dream began coming back to him. Before long, it was all he could think about. Amy was in the office playing catch-up on a project for work. He could hear her typing away as he got up and walked to the doorway to steal her attention. "Hun, I had another dream last night. This one was truly bizarre and literally out of this world."

Before he could describe the vision, she interrupted him, "Oh! Speaking of dreams, that reminds me! That book finally came in that I ordered for you, the one on lucid dreaming! Remember?"

The thought was a welcome distraction. Thomas had become enthralled with his increase in dream activity lately and wanted to learn more about the possibilities of controlling them. "Oh, yeah! I forgot! I've got some studying to do tonight then!"

She handed him the package that was sitting on the edge of her desk and said, "Have fun!" Thomas hurried back to the couch like a little kid with a shiny new toy on Christmas. He put the cartoons on mute and opened the book to the first chapter. To his dismay, it was on meditation, a practice he had up to this point labeled as pseudoscience.

Great, he thought to himself, but he was willing to implement any and every teaching the book could offer if it meant enhancing his dreaming experience.

Giving it the old college try, he read about finding a quiet spot to relax and focus on emptying the mind. He read about the benefits of living in the now and not dwelling in the past nor the future. To Thomas, it all sounded fine and dandy, but he knew the "emptying the mind" part would prove to be the most difficult. To be called an overactive thinker would be considered an understatement for him in particular. Nonetheless, he headed to the bedroom and closed the door; he sat on the bed and began trying to implement some of the proper techniques he had read about. Some of which were sitting cross-legged and keeping his back straight, while others included breathing deeply and focusing on each breath.

Inhale… exhale… over and over. He could manage to focus on nothingness but only for a few seconds at a time. After twenty minutes of practicing, frustration and hopelessness began to set in, but he remained persistent. Slowly, with each exhale, he began to let go of certain elements of stress that were clouding his mind. One by one, they left him. His heart rate slowed. His breathing deepened. His mind was clear.

After a few more minutes, or hours for all he knew, colors and glowing flashes of light began to form in the darkness behind his eyelids. A warmth flowed through his body, and he was filled with a sense of peace and calm. Images from his dreams began to present themselves, like the mighty oak tree and the Deer. He saw a beautiful landscape filled with every color imaginable, but something unnerving caught his attention behind the tree line. A shadowy figure lurked just out of sight in his vision. It drew more and more attention as Thomas tried to focus on it.

In a whirlwind, it made its sinister presence known and consumed the landscape in a black mist until every ounce of beauty had been covered in darkness. Thomas' heart rate began to climb as he tried to make sense of this new void and the ominous being responsible. His mind had returned to nothingness and silence, but before he gave up on the meditation, a set of glowing red eyes opened face-to-face with him, and one word was seared into his brain by a terrifying voice, *LIAR!* Thomas was jolted back to full consciousness, heart racing and sweating profusely.

"What the hell was that?" he said under labored breathing. After composing himself, he realized the sun had gone down and hours passed by without him realizing. *I must have fallen asleep!* he thought to himself as he left the bedroom.

Amy was already sleeping on the couch and sleeping hard. Thomas knew she was exhausting herself with work and needed the rest. He brought her an extra blanket and draped it over her legs. She looked so comfortable, and a little stream of drool was puddling on her pillow. He grinned and quietly headed back to the bedroom. Even though he felt like he just woke up from a serious nap, he was still very sleepy, drained even. The bed was calling his name as he crawled under the covers and rested his head on the pillow. Before long, he was drifting off…

The glare of a bright light subsided, and Thomas found himself standing in the gorgeous land he had seen in meditation. The sun beat down on his face and sweat dripped from the tip of his nose. He had a bow in hand, carved from the branch of a juniper tree, and the string pulled full draw. He focused on the tree line only twenty yards away. His muscles trembled as he held on with the last bit of strength he had left.

Thomas was starving, and his eyes widened when the sound of a snapping twig caught his attention. He brought the nock of the arrow to the corner of his eye and held his breath. In an instant, the Deer from his dreams emerged from the brush and looked directly at him. His heart sank, but he kept his bow drawn as they stared at each other. After a moment of contemplation, and despite his insatiable hunger, Thomas lowered the bow and loosened his grip on the string.

He was relieved he hadn't fired, as the Deer slowly approached. His snout dipped toward the ground to nibble on a patch of grass before raising his antlers high and conveying another telepathic message, *The pure hearted stays his hand, but he must search with more than eyes to find the nourishment he needs.*

Thomas bent to one knee in respect for the creature, knowing very well that this could be the

voice of God as he knew Him. "What nourishment am I supposed to be searching for?" he asked.

The Deer turned and slowly headed back to the tree line before sending its last message, *Your spirit is what starves, not your body, not your mind.*

Thomas thought to himself, *Well, that's hardly useful... How am I supposed to feed my spirit?* but the Deer had vanished, and a familiar dark energy had taken its place. He looked around frantically with his bow readied, then the hairs on the back of his neck stood on end when the sound of heavy footsteps came barreling up behind him. He turned to draw his bow, but it was too late. A black mass of evil with glowing red eyes blasted through him like a bolt of lightning. It sent him hurtling backwards and crashing into the ground like a ragdoll. He stared at the sky, with no wind in his lungs as the cold, black air surrounded him. Then it devoured him.

As if being summoned from the dead, Thomas sat up in bed and drew a deep, raspy breath to fill his empty lungs. He was still shaking from the dream he just had and closed his eyes to calm down. *It was just a dream,* he told himself. "Not a good start to this lucid dreaming stuff," he chuckled as his heart rate began to settle, but upon opening his eyes, he realized that something was definitely still wrong.

The wall color had changed in his bedroom, and the unfamiliar sound of barking came from the other side of the door. Thomas made his way out of the bedroom when a large black and white pitbull came charging toward him. The dog jumped up to his shoulders and licked his face, almost toppling him. "Hun! Where did this dog come from?! Tell me you didn't adopt this beast without talking to me first!" shouted Thomas.

His wife shouted back from the couch, "Haha, very funny coming from the one who picked him!"

The dog lowered to all fours and ran back into the living room. Thomas raised an eyebrow and walked down the hall to find that the entire layout of the house had changed. "AMY! What the hell is going on?! Have you been working on this all night?"

She glared at him with suspicion and asked, "First of all, who's Amy? And second, working on what?"

He replied, "The furniture! And the wall color! You even tore up that old carpet! And Amy is your damn name, isn't it?"

Her stare of suspicion turned to confusion, "Hun, calm down, you're starting to scare me, my name is Katie, you know that."

Thomas' eyes fluttered in the exchange before he put his hands in the air and slowly walked toward the kitchen mumbling under his breath, "This is a dream… this is a dream…"

He poured himself a glass of water as his wife said in a calm voice, "We painted and rearranged the furniture together six months ago, remember?"

He couldn't help but laugh a bit before responding, "Sure, hun…"

A few moments turned into a good while of Thomas pacing back and forth in the kitchen, becoming more and more desperate as time passed. He was sure he was dreaming, but his surroundings seemed all too real. He convinced himself that he would wake up, but when? He had just about enough of dreaming lately and tried pinching himself, but nothing worked. He could hear "Katie" in the living room, humming some melody he didn't recognize and decided that if he was dreaming, then he might as well make the most of it. Thomas walked back into the living room after calming down and sat on the couch with Katie and the dog, who climbed into his lap. He scratched behind the dog's ears as he tried to relax and collect himself. Thomas rubbed his chin and realized that a week's worth of scruff had grown on his face.

The details and vividness of his surroundings caused him to forget he was dreaming, but only for a moment as another state of confusion set in. "Wait a minute! Isn't it Monday? This was supposed to be my first day back at work! How could you let me sleep in?!" Thomas exclaimed to Katie.

She didn't even look at him before responding, "You know damn well you lost that job weeks ago. That company went bankrupt."

Weeks?! he thought to himself, but it helped him snap back to the idea that he was dreaming. Thomas convinced himself that his head was fine and the injury he sustained had long since healed. The minutes turned into hours as he became restless and agitated.

"That's it!" he shouted, as he jumped off the couch in a frenzy. "It's time to wake up! Let me off the ride! I don't want to play anymore!" he shouted again as he began slapping himself over and over in the hopes of returning to his reality.

"Kevin, stop it! Calm down, you're scaring Boone!" Katie yelled at him.

Thomas continued stomping around like a lunatic, screaming, "I've been dreaming on the raaaaail road! ALL THE LIVE LONG DAY!!! Wake up... wake up! WAKE UP!!!" Boone started barking aggressively as Thomas began punching holes in the drywall. CRACK! A bone popped in his right hand.

"Kevin! Please stop!" Katie shouted again.

"MY NAME IS NOT KEVIN!" he shouted back, and with that, Boone charged forward and latched on to Thomas' arm as he let out a growl of his own. The adrenaline was pumping like a steam engine, and Thomas snatched his bleeding arm out of the dog's jaws long enough to run down the hall and lock himself in the bedroom.

"I'm calling the police!" Katie shouted as he grabbed the reading chair in the corner and wedged it under the doorknob. Thomas ignored the barking and frantic phone call on the other side of the door. He jumped on the bed cross-legged in one final attempt to wake up.

Maybe the key isn't waking up but going back to sleep! he thought. He closed his eyes and tried with all his might to clear his mind. Breath after breath, his heart rate wasn't slowing, and the blood flowed from his arm and hand like a sieve. He focused, and the barking began to fade. *Breathe,* he thought to himself, *Just breathe.* Before long, he was concentrating on the darkness and silence of his mind, and the glow of familiar colors and shapes came to him.

The shape of the Deer showed itself once more, but it was blurry. Thomas wanted nothing more than to get off his rollercoaster ride of a dream, so he focused on the shape of the creature, praying it would show him the way. The silhouette sharpened, and for a moment, the creature was clear to him. To his dismay, the animal was wounded and bloodied, with an arrow protruding from its left shoulder. The sorrow he felt for the creature was real, and in a few seconds, the shadow of his nightmare crept up from behind and pounced on his antlered messenger with the jaws of a lion. Thomas was startled and his focus was broken. The adrenaline was wearing off and searing pain tore through his arm and hand.

Then a loud banging echoed through the door. "Police! We're coming in!" Thomas heard the warning and the shuffling of multiple officers preparing to break the door down. He frantically ran to the bedroom window for a quick escape, but it was too late. A loud crash splintered the door and frame, breaking the legs of the chair and sending it sliding across the floor.

"Bring it on, dream police!" Thomas yelled, preparing for a valiant showdown with the law, but before he could even raise his fists, a maple gunstock struck him between the eyes. He folded backward and collapsed to the floor like a limp noodle. He got what he asked for – the dream was over, but the nightmare was just beginning.

Chapter 10
Rude Awakening

Journey's over, battle won,
The war and dream have just begun.

Kevin opened his eyes to the brightest, whitest place he had ever seen. Thankfully, the light wasn't blinding, in fact, it was warm and welcoming. However, there was nothing there. No floor, no ceiling, no walls. Just a blank canvas. "Am I dead? Is this Heaven?" Kevin questioned his new circumstances. "Wait… how could I be dead if I've been dreaming this whole time?" He thought back on the stone he came across in the forest path and tried to discern what it meant one last time:

A man with no path, has no name,
He disregards life, and lives in shame,

He struggled through his patchy understanding of the rhyme and kept getting stuck on the last line. "Does that mean… I've failed? If it wasn't a dream, and I'm actually dead, what was I supposed to do differently? Was any of this real? Or was I never even alive in the first place?"

A familiarly booming voice came from behind him, "You were dead in life, but now you are alive in death and in all things as I am. Do not fret, Kevin, you have done very well, but you are not finished." Kevin turned, expecting to see the Deer, but there was nothing and the voice continued. "There is another on the path, and you must help him complete his journey as well."

Kevin paused before responding. He looked up into the void and said, "I will do whatever you ask of me, but answer me this one question. In this dream, I died once before in the forest and afterward, I just woke up in the same forest and in the same dream. Why does this feel different? Did I spend all my lives, like in a video game? Am I really dead?"

The voice boomed again, "I said before, you are alive but your old life is dead and gone. Those on the path must travel it until they reach the end, no matter how many mistakes they make along the way. No matter how long it takes, everyone reaches the end."

These words from the voice in the void made Kevin think about Jacob in the forest, living the same hunt over and over for decades. *Great…* he thought to himself.

"Do not worry about Jacob, you two will reach the end together, but first you must help another." The void replied as if reading his thoughts. Without hesitation, Kevin responded, "Here am I, send me…"

Thomas awoke to the feeling of something soft brushing past his fingertips. Blood was still dripping from the tip of his nose and trickling past his wrist. He opened his eyes to the sight of a wall of dead grass passing by, like being swept away by a giant push broom. A lumpy surface underneath him dipped and swayed from side to side. The surface was velvety on his cheek and smelled like pine.

He was draped like a saddle over the back of his dream guide, the Deer that had been reaching out to him. "Uuughhhh… where am I?" he mumbled as he raised his head to soak up his surroundings.

On the path, the Deer said to him. He was being carried through a dried-up field of tall grass, and they were headed for what looked like a giant canyon off in the distance.

Thomas raised himself up and swung one leg over the Deer to get more comfortable. He looked around and asked, "Where are you taking me?"

The Deer dipped his antlers over to the left, and the black marble of an eye on the side of his head looked back at him. *I am taking you to the past and the future – to what must be seen and not forgotten*, the Deer replied.

"Man, oh man, you really love those riddles, don't you? Can I call you Henry? You look like a Henry to me," Thomas said. The Deer remained silent as he trotted along. "Henry it is…" Thomas said under his breath. There was still a dull ache pounding away in his forehead from the gun butt. "So, have I finally lost my mind? Or am I just sleeping? And if I'm sleeping, please wake me up… this lucid dreaming mess is exhausting."

In a way, you are sleeping, yes… but it will be a long time before you wake up, the Deer replied.

What does that mean? Thomas thought to himself as he rubbed his head. As they went along, the air was getting hotter, and the sky was darkening. They were getting closer to the canyon, and Thomas noticed a commotion by the edge of the rocky cliff. He could make out a man standing toe-to-toe with a mirrored shadow of himself and a woman with dark hair caring for another man on the ground.

"What's happening over there, Henry? Who

is that?" Thomas pointed out.

This is what you must see, the end of one path and the beginning of another... the Deer responded. The red sun was beginning to settle on the horizon, when the edge of the field was set ablaze in an instant.

"Whoa! What was that?!" Thomas yelled. He gazed through the flames as the man attacked the shadow, only to be cast into the dust. He rose and was cast down again, over and over the man gathered himself and charged forward, but his pace slowed with each blow he took. "We need to help him!" Thomas shouted as he watched the shadow dance effortlessly around the man.

This is his fight, one only he can win, the Deer said to him. Thomas looked on in horror as the beast allowed one final attempt before striking the man down for good.

This is a nightmare... I can't watch this! Thomas thought to himself.

You must... the Deer spoke within him.

The shadow slowly approached the man writhing on the ground, using what energy he could muster to rise once more, but he couldn't. He pushed off the ground and could only settle to his knees. Thomas could see the man was bloodied with head hung low and he knew this was the end, but the creature didn't attack. Instead, he watched as the shadow extended one of its gangly claws, as if to help him to his feet. The man slowly looked up at the beast and there was a pause and what looked like a brief dialogue between the two.

"What is happening?" Thomas asked.

The Deer's answer gave him chills, *The choice.*

The man slowly reached toward the demon's offering, but he didn't take it. In the blink of an eye, the man raised his blade with his other hand and plunged it into his own chest.

The creature let out a deafening screech as it hunched over, twitching and convulsing in pain. At that exact moment, Thomas felt a searing pain tear through his own chest as he gasped and grabbed at the phantom wound. The screeching got louder and higher pitched before the beast collapsed in front of the stranger. As it violently shook, new appendages started sprouting from its sides and back, one by one, an arm and then a leg, then another arm and another leg, until it appeared to be morphing and splitting into three different beings. A new head and torso were pulling away on either side of the original shadow, which was now dwindling and wasting away. Despite his agony, Thomas couldn't look away as the man with the knife in his chest gave his last breath and toppled to his side. With that, the screeching ceased, and the demon exploded with a massive shockwave of dark energy and lightning, sending glowing embers into the field.

The two spawned beings were sent hurtling in opposite directions, and the blast sent Thomas flying through the air. He rolled and flipped through the grass that was burning all around him before sliding to a stop almost twenty feet away. Dazed and shaken, Thomas sat up in a panic, realizing he couldn't hear anything. He was shell shocked, and the fight or flight response was kicking in, but the Deer was nowhere to be seen. Thomas got up and started running back the way they came, stumbling over tufts of grass and his own feet before clearing the flames.

Even though he couldn't hear anything, he could feel the evil presence pursuing him as he sprinted away from the catastrophe. The shadows had rallied and were hot on his heels as he looked back over his shoulder to see them tearing through the burning field. They came full speed like a couple of cheetahs, snuffing out the flames as they passed by. Before he could even turn his head to see where he was going, a new, strange voice shouted at him from within his mind, *Look out!*

It was too late. Thomas lost his footing and fell forward into a massive black pit in the ground that hadn't been there before. He slammed into the other side of the pit and desperately grabbed and clawed at the ground, trying to hold on. The tufts of grass tore from the earth and slipped through his fingers as he went over the edge. He couldn't even hear his own screams as he plummeted into the darkness.

Hey, Tommy boy, wake up... hey, man, get up! WAKE UP!!! echoed and bounced around his head as Thomas opened his eyes. He was face down, drooling in the dirt in a new world.

"Waa… what? Who said that? Who's there?" he asked as he wiped the dirt and drool from one side of his face and raised his head to gaze upon a beautiful garden. Locked in bewilderment at the sight of such a place for a brief moment, Thomas looked around to take it all in. The flowering trees, the berry bushes, the warmth of the sun – it all seemed vaguely familiar. He couldn't help but feel like he had been there before. "Well, at least this dream is finally getting better," he said aloud.

Pretty, isn't it? Thomas heard in the back of his head.

He sprang to his feet and spun around in a flash, shouting, "Who's there?!" but there was no one behind him.

Over here! came from behind him again, but still, no one. The hairs rose on the back of Thomas' neck. *Calm down, Tommy boy, my name is Kevin, and I'm pretty sure you just watched me die. Thanks for the*

help by the way... I know you've met our mutual friend with the antlers, the voice said.

"My gosh, that was you? Henry told me we couldn't help you but I wanted to. I'm not sure what that was all about, but for what it's worth, you went down like a hero, in a true blaze of glory. Now, why can't I see you? Where are you?" Thomas responded as he looked around once more.

The voice chimed in again, *Thanks, I appreciate it, but it was meant to be. I thought my journey had come to an end, but it seems my path is intertwined with yours now, according to the Deer, anyway. After it all happened, I found myself in a white void. There was no sound, or gravity for that matter, but that Deer appeared and explained a few things to me. Don't freak out, but I'm... in your head.*

"Wait... in my head?! Why?! For how long?! Get out!" Thomas exclaimed.

No can do, buddy; believe me, I'm not happy about it either. These dreams... what's been happening to both of us, I thought I was just crazy. Now I know for certain that there's much more to this than I originally thought. The Deer kept saying there was something I was supposed to accomplish before I could be free of this hell and I thought saving my friends from that evil that had been stalking me was it, but it was only part of it. I still don't know what it is, but he did say we are supposed to work together to find out. I promise you're not crazy either, Kevin responded.

"No, you don't understand, man, I'm just dreaming, I've been practicing meditation in order to lucid dream. I'm not going to lie, this has been the worst, most bizarre dream I've ever had, but still, it's only a dream. I'm going to wake up and be just fine," Thomas said.

If you say so, Tommy boy. The fact of the matter is, everything you thought you knew about yourself, about your life, about everything... you might as well throw all that crap straight out the window. The faster you get used to that, the better off you're going to be, trust me. The good news is, there's a gift for you that should make your journey easier – it definitely came in handy for me on more than one occasion, Kevin said in a calm tone.

"A gift?" Thomas asked as the sound of rustling came from a row of wild blueberry bushes. He was startled as a curled set of horns emerged from the bushes. It was a large ram carrying a set of leather bags. His mind was set at ease, at least it wasn't one of those dark creatures that had been chasing him, and the closer the ram got, the more familiar the encounter felt.

Hey, buddy! Long time no see! You're gonna love this, Tommy, Kevin exclaimed inside Thomas' mind. The ram approached and knelt down so the harness and baggage could slide off his shoulders and past his curly horns, resting on the ground at Thomas' feet.

"What is this stuff? And why do I feel like I've seen it before?" Thomas asked Kevin.

Go on, take a look and find out, he answered. Thomas knelt down to examine the gear. He saw the bone handle of the same hunting knife Kevin was wielding in his showdown with the beast. He also noticed the cattle horn, which was the most familiar out of all the gear, and the backpack with a silvery material protruding from the top. His eye caught the glint of condensation on the small water skin.

"Man, oh man, is this water? I'm thirsting to death!" Thomas said as he grabbed it, uncorked the top, and took a big gulp. "Man… ice-cold. That's the best water I've ever had! Thank you!" Thomas said to the ram.

He doesn't speak, not like the Deer anyway. This ram brought me all of this gear when I first set foot on the path. The horn is from my childhood, a distinct memory I hold onto, but now it feels more like a dream than a memory. Like an illusion – I know it happened but it might not necessarily have been my memory. Anyways, it's yours now so take care of it, Kevin said. Thomas gathered everything, buckled the belt around his waist, and threw the bag over his shoulder while the ram slowly turned and made his way back toward the bushes. He was headed up a worn path that wound upwards through the hills and straight toward a solitary mountain peak covered in snow, miles and miles away.

Thomas spent the next several hours exploring the landscape and conversing with Kevin. He asked Kevin about the silvery mesh and the rest of the gear. He asked about the people he was with at the end. Thomas asked about everything and Kevin answered with what answers he had. Thomas was getting closer and closer to an understanding he didn't realize he was searching for, but the closer he got, the more unnerved he felt. What he thought was only a dream was turning out to be a whole new reality he was a part of. But how? And why?

The sun was beginning to go down and Thomas' eyes were getting heavy. "So how does this work? Do I just go back to sleep to wake up? Where will I be?" he asked Kevin.

That's something I never quite figured out myself. Losing consciousness was definitely what sent me somewhere, but the where, why, and how always seemed to change. Also, every time I woke up, I lost more and more time. So be ready for that, Tommy boy, Kevin replied.

Thomas spotted a small patch of soft moss on the edge of one of the paths and stretched out for a rest. He clasped his hands behind his head and gazed up at the stars that were beginning to shine while the sky darkened. "How much time am I going to lose?" he asked.

It's all kind of blurry for me looking back on

the timeline, but at one point I lost two years… Just remember: Your life, who you were, and what you perceive as reality is simply an illusion. I know that's hard to wrap your head around, but time is a bit irrelevant now. I promise it will all start to make more sense. Just give it… TIME! HAHAHA! Sorry, I couldn't help myself! Kevin responded.

Thomas furrowed his brow at the less than desirable answer and thought to himself, *What the heck does that mean? This guy sounds like a lunatic… and now he's stuck in my head? Great…*

Kevin blurted out, *I HEARD THAT…*

Thomas' eyes widened from embarrassment and answered, "You can read my thoughts too?!"

Kevin said, *Yes, and I can see what you imagine, so do me a favor and don't think of anything gross… or scary… or just anything unpleasant in general. It's a lot more vivid for me up here. I know this isn't ideal, but we have to work together to figure this all out. What do you say? Partners?"*

Thomas calmed down, watching the stars getting brighter and brighter. He stretched his arms out and let out a deep yawn. Before his eyelids closed and he drifted off to sleep, he responded, "Partners."

Oh man! Oh man! Oh man! Here we go!!! Kevin yelled as Thomas was startled awake. He opened his eyes as they were hurtling past the stars. *OH YEAH!!! I REMEMBER THIS!* Kevin shouted again as they picked up momentum.

"Yeah?! Me... me, too! Didn't care for it much the first time!" Thomas replied in a nervous voice. They were flying straight toward the moon. It was getting bigger and bigger, but they weren't slowing down.

Uuuuuhhhhh! I don't remember this part! Kevin yelled before they both screamed as they collided with the surface of the moon faster than sound. **CRASH!** The sound of shattering glass echoed around them, and although they were still being pulled through time and space, their travel had slowed tremendously. A bright light blinded Thomas upon smashing through the moon as he floated inwards.

Wooo! What a rush! Thomas, open your eyes, man; I can't see anything, Kevin said.

"I can't! It's too bright... I'm not sure where we are, but I think we're floating," Thomas responded. The light around them was warm and gave off a peaceful energy that Kevin and Thomas both recognized.

Are we finally dead, Tommy boy? Kevin asked. Thomas didn't reply right away, he was too enamored with the feeling at hand. It was complete and total bliss. He could feel every ounce of negative energy being transferred away and being replaced with the goodness that surrounded him, and for some reason, he knew that everything was going to be okay.

"Something tells me we aren't getting off that easy," Thomas answered.

Though he couldn't see, the silence around them broke with a faint, fast-paced beeping that got louder and louder. *Where is that coming from?* Thomas thought to himself, but before Kevin could chime in, the sound of two muffled voices could be heard between the beeping. They sounded concerned, and whatever they were saying quickly escalated into an argument.

Tommy boy, I'm out of my depth here. I'm not sure what's happening, Kevin noted. The booming beeps went from a fast-paced pattern, to a steady, solid tone. It was now a loud humming that seemed to be coming from everywhere. The sound caused a vibration they could both feel, and Thomas' heart began to race, with adrenaline making its way into his veins. His toes and fingertips started to tingle as one word could be made out over the echoing hum.

"CLEAR!" was shouted at them from the void. In a matter of seconds, the once blinding light flipped into darkness, and the loud hum began to fade away.

Thomas slowly opened his eyes to get a look at his surroundings, when a paralyzing jolt of electricity came blasting out of his chest, locking his joints in place. Tongues of lightning were tethered to his body and whipped back and forth, illuminating the spherical inside of the moon with blue light. Though he felt no pain, the terror struck Thomas deeply, and as fast as the blue light exploded, it was snuffed into darkness by the booming crash of thunder that trailed off into silence.

Another crack of thunder rumbled in the deep, then silence. Another softer boom echoed in the dark before Thomas began snapping out of a detached form of consciousness. His eyes were open, but his vision was blurred with glowing streaks of gray and blue light, like the first few strokes of a Jackson Pollock painting. He couldn't think. With no baseline to initiate even the smallest of thought processes. A sudden flash of light, followed by one more boom of thunder that rolled off into nothingness.

The muffled voices were coming back into focus, but they were coming from different people now.

No, no, no, NO, NO! Tommy boy, snap out of it! We've got a problem!

Thomas recognized Kevin's voice in his head, but he couldn't comprehend what the word "problem" even meant. It felt like the very fabric of his mind had been shredded down to fraying threads. The more he tried to discern the situation at hand, the harder it became. Things like his age, name, and any short-term memory were completely blank.

C'mon, Tommy boy! Wake up! I need you! Kevin shouted at him again.

A glowing column of white light passed across Thomas' field of vision from right to left and with it one of the voices became clearer. The other remained behind him somewhere.

Thomas! Listen to me… we are trapped and I don't know where we are. If you can hear me, try to blink your eyes, and wiggle your toes, Kevin said.

Slowly but surely, Thomas began collecting his senses. His vision started clearing up and he could tell he was sitting in a chair facing a blue table with a few files and a cup full of pens on it. A large fluorescent light fixture was shining down on the table, and the room was lined with gray cinder block walls.

I… I can't move, Kevin… what's happening to me? Thomas pleaded.

I hate to say it, Tommy boy, but we might be in a hospital. The kind where they stick you with a horse tranquilizer when you step out of line. Believe it or not, this isn't my first rodeo, but last time I was able to use my legs, so we're going to have to work together to figure this out. I'm not exactly sure what the next move is, but the only thing I know for certain is that if they give you a pill, try not to swallow it, Kevin replied.

At that moment, the voice to his left spoke up, "Looks like he might be waking up…"

The one behind him replied, "Don't worry, I've got another dose ready to go if he flips out again."

"How are you feeling today, Thomas? That was quite the show you put on for us yesterday. You must be exhausted!" the voice to his left said.

Thomas' vision was finally clearing up enough to see the white silhouette was a man in a doctor's coat, standing at the far end of the blue table in front of him. "You know, ever since you came to us, you've made your recovery as difficult as possible. Don't you know that all we want is to help you?"

Thomas tried to reply, but all that came out was a groan and a stream of drool. The two voices continued to make small talk and banter back and forth in the background. His skin was warm and tingly, but he noticed he was regaining the ability to move his fingertips.

Kevin chimed in, *Man! They've really done a number on you, haven't they! You must have really given them hell if they had to pull out the sleepy darts. Do you remember anything? Like how you might have ended up here in the first place?*

I think I got in a fight with the cops… I'm not sure, I thought it was part of the dream. I had woken up, but everything was just a little different than it was before, and my wife was somebody else. Wait... in fact, she called me Kevin! Is your wife's name Katie? Thomas responded.

Yes! You saw my Katie?! How was she? Did you see my boy?! My gosh it's been so long since I've seen them... Kevin asked.

She seemed fine, and if by "boy" you mean the wild beast that almost took my arm off, then yes, I saw him. What a trip! It's like our consciences bled over into one another's. That whole time I thought I was losing my mind inside a dream. Henry may have been right about our paths being linked in some way after all, Thomas responded.

Trust me, after seeing what I've seen, that Deer could tell me the sky is green and I'd believe him. He seems to be the only positive reinforcement I've gotten on this crazy journey. Even after death, I'm still tied to this path, and now our paths are linked. For a split second, I thought I was free... but my work isn't finished yet... Also, if Boone actually bit you, that means you deserved it, Kevin replied.

Thomas heard the sound of a door opening behind him, and a third voice saying, "Hey, someone is here to see Thomas and she's not happy about the sedation... apparently, he was supposed to be transferred to a research facility months ago. I'll stall her as long as I can, but this lady is PISSED, and she has credentials…"

"What?! Are you kidding me? Who dropped the ball on this?! Keep her busy… I'll think of something," the man replied. Thomas could hear the visitor leave abruptly and close the door behind him.

"I bet it was Pam… she can't even schedule appointments right," the voice behind remarked.

"If I find out it's her, she's gone… I could lose my license over this shit. Go get me the wake-up kit," the man replied.

As the second voice made a similarly swift exit, Kevin whispered, *No way…* but before Thomas could think to ask what he meant, the man in front of him leaned in closer across the table for Thomas' vision to sharpen up just enough to get a good look at the man who seemed to be in charge. He was wearing a doctor's coat, with thick framed glasses and a large bandage on the right side of his face.

He said, "It looks like this might be your lucky day. If you know what's good for you, you'll keep your mouth shu—" he was cut off by the sound of a commotion on the other side of the door. The sound of a woman on a mission came echoing down the hall, scolding and threatening like a screeching banshee at any soul unlucky enough to cross her path.

IT IS! Kevin shouted in Thomas' mind.

What? What the hell is going on? Thomas

asked, but before he could get a response, the door swung open and the woman stormed in, causing the villainous figure to retract like a snake back in its hole.

The woman shouted, "Did you think you were going to get away with this?! What kind of facility are you running here?! I've got you figured out, Kellen! You snuffed me out of my own research for your financial gain, and now you're trying to steal my patients? I guess the pharmaceutical scam wasn't enough, huh?"

The man attempted a timid response, "Ma'am, I'm not sure who…" but he was cut off again by the tongue of wrath.

"Leave me with my patient at once!"

The man tried one more time, "Ma'am, you can't just…"

"AT ONCE!" she snapped, slamming her fist on the table in front of him. With that, the doctor slowly slinked out of the room, tail tucked between his legs, and closed the door.

We're gonna be okay, Tommy boy! We're getting out of here! Kevin exclaimed.

Thomas, in shock from the last few moments, stayed quiet. The woman took a deep breath and exhaled. Still very much paralyzed, Thomas noticed his chair being rotated to the right, and the woman knelt down in front of him. She was beautiful, with long, black hair in a ponytail and the edge of a tattoo creeping up her neck past her white collar.

Even though Thomas couldn't feel anything, he knew the hairs on the back of his neck were standing straight up again when she said four simple words that would change him forever:

"We need to talk…"